GREYGLASS

GREYGLASS

Tanith Lee

Stafford England

Greyglass
By Tanith Lee
© 2011

This is a work of fiction. All the characters and events portrayed in this book are fictitious, and any resemblance to real people, or events, is purely coincidental.

All rights reserved, including the right to reproduce this book, or portions thereof, in any form.

The right of Tanith Lee to be identified as the author of this work has been asserted by her in accordance with the Copyright, Design and Patents Act, 1988.

http://www.tanithlee.com

Cover by John Kaiine
Layout by Storm Constantine

Set in Palatino Linotype

ISBN 978-1-907737-04-6

IP0099

An Immanion Press Edition
8 Rowley Grove
Stafford ST17 9BJ
http://www.immanion-press.com
info@immanion-press.com

BOOKS BY TANITH LEE

A Selection from her 93 titles

The Birthgrave Trilogy (The Birthgrave; Vazkor, son of Vazkor, Quest for the White Witch)

The Vis Trilogy (The Storm Lord; Anackire; The White Serpent)

The Flat Earth Opus (Night's Master; Death's Master; Delusion's Master; Delirium's Mistress; Night's Sorceries)

Don't Bite the Sun

Drinking Sapphire Wine

The Paradys Quartet (The Book of the Damned; The Book of the Beast; The Book of the Dead; The Book of the Mad)

The Venus Quartet (Faces Under Water; Saint Fire; A Bed of Earth; Venus Preserved)

Sung in Shadow

A Heroine of the World

The Scarabae Blood Opera (Dark Dance; Personal Darkness; Darkness, I)

The Blood of Roses

When the Lights Go Out

Heart-Beast

Elephantasm

Reigning Cats and Dogs

The Unicorn Trilogy (Black Unicorn; Gold Unicorn; Red Unicorn)

The Claidi Journals (Law of the Wolf Tower; Wolf Star Rise, Queen of the Wolves, Wolf Wing)

The Piratica Novels (Piratica 1; Piratica 2; Piratica 3)

The Silver Metal Lover

Metallic Love

The Gods Are Thirsty

Collections

Nightshades
Dreams of Dark and Light
Red As Blood – Tales From the Sisters Grimmer
Tamastara, or the Indian Nights
The Gorgon
Tempting the Gods
Hunting the Shadows
Sounds and Furies

Book One

I

She lived in a vegetable house. As time passed, it grew about her. Rooms and passages added themselves, stairways, attics, cellars; windows formed. Outside, and all around, the gardens also extended into mossy terraces with pools, massive stands of huge trees, thickets of rhododendrons. Where visible through these, the house appeared like an orange pumpkin – the one in Cinderella perhaps, which became a coach to take her to the ball. However, the house was only volatile in an accretive, sedentary way, adding to itself, certainly determined not to move anywhere else.

"We're going up to see the old lady now. Put your coat on. Hurry up."

Susan glanced at her mother, and laid down the nail scissors with which she had been cutting figures of thin paper.

"Are those my nail scissors?"

"_ _ _"

"I said, are those my nail scissors?"

Whose nail scissors, after all, could they be?

"Yes, Mum."

"Don't call me Mum."

"_ _ _"

"Say Mummy."

"Mummy."

"I've told you not to use the nail scissors for that. It spoils them."

Susan looked at the spoiled scissors. They appeared the same as when she had taken them from the bathroom cabinet half an hour ago, as her mother was peeling vegetables for – don't say dinner, say lunch – lunch.

"Go and put your coat on. Will you hurry, Susan!"

Susan ran out. She was twelve. For a year she had been menstruating regularly, using deodorant and mascara, and wearing tights. She felt twenty, then fifteen. Then eight. Even between one running step and another she might change.

Her mother was calling again. Susan had been supposed to put on her school blazer from the hall. But Susan ran into her bedroom and took up the jacket from her chair. In the mirror, as she passed, she glimpsed a plump ugly girl, with short fair hair, who, sometimes, by careful arrangements of light and shade, the mirror and herself, might be transformed into something else, someone of consequence, even perhaps attraction.

"Susan! What are you doing?"

"I don't want to go up *there*," said Susan, to the corner of the room. The corner did not reply.

It was spring outside. More spring than had yet got into the year, or the old building, or the flat on the second floor. The Georgian pillars and porch had burst into slices of sunlight and the steps were warm.

"Why have you put that jacket on, Susan?"
"You said –"
"I said a coat. Your blazer."
But now there was no turning back.

The sun dappled leopard spots through the chestnut trees by the wall. The buds were sticky, still red but not green.

Susan looked at her mother. A slim beautiful woman, a fully-formed creature, at no disadvantage since adult. Her hair, which was black this month, gleamed with a reddish light like that on the chestnut buds.

"Why do we have to?"
"What? Why do we have to what?"
"Go up *there*."
"You know why. You know perfectly well why."
"But –"
"And we're late."

They walked quickly along Constance Street, where the tree roots had here and there upheaved the pavement, and into Dunkirk Street, where there were no trees and the sun fell hot, burning on their heads.

"You brushed your hair," said the adult woman.
"Mmm."

Susan had not, what a bit of luck.

Sundays would be all right, if it weren't for this – this, and the approaching shadow of school tomorrow, but that was almost a whole day away.

"Oh damn, we're so late. Come on."

In at the park gates. People were strolling about. There was a van selling ice-cream. Dogs rushed barking, and somewhere children screamed, and a big blast of exciting drum-thick bad music roared from a radio on the lawns.

"Bloody music," said Susan's mother. "People."

They were almost running now.

Straight through the park, with its possibilities of life, straight along the gravel path by the black, still-winter beds, a handful of crocuses and anaemic daffodils, and out of the other gate.

Here was ominous, curving Tower Road, with its enormous beech trees and oaks, its gardens behind ten-foot stone walls clung with ivy. Set far back, roofs of houses showed, like the upper turrets of the Sleeping Beauty's castle.

"Mum, I've got a stitch."

"Mummy. Damn, it's ten past twelve. Oh damn."

"Why do we have to *go*? You don't want to. She just goes on."

The road curving and coiling, like an ancient riverbed, slid in under the trees, cold now in the fragmented shade, heavy as smashed masonry, sky watery as broken blue eggs. And now, landmarks, plants lodged in a wall. A turn, a gap where grass grew, rather long for the time of year, and the two particular oaks, sentinels which marked the border of the witch's kingdom.

Her mother pushed the tall, old and rusty ironwork gate, and pushed herself and Susan through it.

"*Why*, Mummy – She doesn't want us here – she doesn't like us."

"No," said Susan's mother, defeated after all, stopping dead, just over the border, there under the weight of cascading evergreens, the overgrown drive running away and away towards the orange pumpkin that was the witch's house.

"Why then?"
"You know why."
"I don't."
"She's your grandmother."

The housekeeper, Mrs Danvers, opened the door. Danvers wasn't really her name. Susan's mother had coined it for her from the character in the book by Daphne du Maurier.

Mrs Danvers was very thin and hard of frame. She seemed made of iron, and then clothed to hide it, just her head and neck and hands, and sometimes her lower arms and calves, if visible, gone over with a flesh substituting material like sallow creased rayon. She was old, over forty. (Susan's mother, also over forty, seemed somehow not old, her few facial lines invisible, her skin and make-up flawless, her hair, now blonde, now black, her eyes large and grey.) But Mrs Danvers had got this all wrong and in reverse, black eyes and grey permed hair.

"She's been waiting," said Mrs Danvers.
"Yes," said Susan's mother, shortly.

The hall was very wide, much wider even than in the house where the flats were. A stained glass panel in the door, once it shut, threw jade and crimson shapes along the old cracked lino which was, apparently, 'dangerous'.

Susan stepped on each of these shapes, to see the colour seep instantly up through her feet and appear instead on the top of her disappointing flat shoes.

But her mother had left Susan.

She had walked forward briskly, into one of the great rooms which opened to one side of the wide hall. This she crossed, and went through another door and vanished into another room.

Mrs Danvers too had moved off. Susan left the shapes and ran after her mother, across two rooms or three, down a step at one or two of the doorways, into a sunken part of the house.

A green-rain light flooded the rooms here, from the bay trees and conifers pressed close to the sides of the house. The old furniture caught the green reflections, shining in a watery way.

"I'm sorry we're late, Mother. I had to dash out to the shop before twelve, everything was hung up."

Susan was not really aware of the irony of this scene, so familiar, not only from repetition, but from similar scenes of her own: the daughter standing before the mother, making lame excuses.

Susan's mother had a mother, but this did not become apparent to Susan until years after. Susan's mother was simply performing an unavoidable ritual before Susan's grandmother – who must always be called Grandmother, not 'gran', 'nan' or any other degrading counterfeit.

The grandmother sat in a window, where a big pot contained a plant with strange scarlet leaves, which Susan had long ago christened Martian Rhubarb.

The grandmother did not turn her head. Her profile stood there against the greened glass like something stamped into a coin.

Mrs Danvers was old, but the grandmother had

passed on into another country. She was no longer human. Which gave her, it seemed, inordinate powers.

"Well," said Susan's mother, "how have you been?"

"She steals from me," said the grandmother.

"No she doesn't," said Susan's mother.

"How would you know? You're never here."

"I am here now."

"Once a fortnight."

"Once a week, Mother. Sometimes more often. But I have a job, Mother, and a child, and I can't always –" the words were bitten out, "do exactly as I want with any spare time I might have."

"Butter," said the grandmother.

"What do you mean, butter? She steals butter?"

"Food. All types of food. What can I do? I have to rely on the woman."

Susan's mother sighed, opened her bag and took out a packet of cigarettes.

"Yes, you may smoke."

"*Thank* you."

Mrs Danvers came back into the room. On a tray she bore two glasses of a pale dry sherry, and one of fizzy lemonade, a dish of nuts and an ashtray. The ashtray she placed at once by the chair of Susan's mother.

"Thank you, Mrs Marks." Marks was Mrs Danvers' real name. But not really, no, never.

Susan took the lemonade, and sat in a chair drinking it like a parched alcoholic. She knew better than to wander about the room. She must stay still, as must her mother, all attention fixed on the old woman.

If Mrs Marks-Danvers was made of iron and a partial covering of rayon, from what substance had the grandmother been created? Her thinness was so acute, every bone in her body had been accentuated, distorted. Her skin was folded and refolded, sewn down in tense appliquéd lines. Her skin was brown, like that of someone tanned, or from a foreign country. Her eyes – her eyes disturbed Susan – they were full of something but not colour. Perhaps they had been grey once, like her mother's.

Mrs Danvers had gone.

"She takes the sherry, too. And the wine. You'd notice, if you stayed for lunch or dinner, that she fills the bottles up with water. Tap water I may add. How is your sherry? No, don't say it's all right, Anne, I know quite well it's watered down."

"Mother, I'm sure it isn't."

"Yes, you're sure of everything, Anne."

"Have it your own way," said Susan's mother, Anne.

"Have it my own way? I have nothing my own way."

"That's ridiculous."

"Look at me. What do I have *my own way*?"

"You have this house, you're well looked after –"

The grandmother broke in here with her usual curt melodramatic laugh. "Oh yes. Oh yes. *Very* well."

"Mother, what am I supposed to do? What can I do?"

"Nothing, of course. You can do nothing. You couldn't possibly move into this house with me."

"I live as near as I am able."

"If you lived in this house, you could give up your job, as you're pleased to call it. The child could have proper clothes instead of the extraordinary things I see her wearing every time I do see her –"

Susan, feeling the terrible eyes turn to her at last, flinched her own away, finding some sudden fascination with the worn Persian carpet under her feet.

"Mother, I've explained all this to you. I simply can't throw everything up on a whim."

"A whim? A whim? To be with your own mother?" There was neither anger nor pleading in the tone, scarcely, now, even any sarcasm. The old, unwhole voice, with its well-educated accent, was devoid of anything but clipped abrasion.

"I like my work," said Susan's mother crisply. "And I like a little independence. God knows, it's a good thing I do."

"What is that supposed to mean?"

"You know perfectly well what it means."

"That you could not rely on me for help."

Susan's mother sat with lips of smooth coral stone.

The grandmother had twisted her lizard profile fully round into the room, her gaze fixed with a blind still ferocity on a row of china ornaments in the black hearth.

Susan put down her empty glass.

She got up, and edged away from the arena's centre.

Absorbed now, they let her do it.

"Can I go and look at the books?" Susan whispered, too low to be heard.

They heard her.

Not glancing at her, the grandmother rapped, "You have only been here five minutes. If you want the lavatory, say so."

"Then may I go to the lavatory?"

"Yes. Wash your hands afterwards."

Humiliated beyond blushing, Susan left the room by another exit.

Along the passage, where other curious plants luxuriated in narrow winding spaces, Susan heard the voices still. "I have never asked you for anything." "I have never refused you anything." "There were always terms. Impossible ones." Susan heard this conversation, or dialogues of the same kind, on most Sundays.

She opened the lavatory door and went in.

The lavatory was quite big, for what it was. The suite, if so it could be called, a dingy white, both toilet and bowl and hand basin verdigris-stained, with long hairs of cracks. The hot tap did not run hot, nor even warm. In winter, Susan had sometimes marvelled to find its issue felt colder than that of the cold tap.

Before drying her hands, Susan scooped a handful of water up on to the runner of the towel, to make it very wet, proving she had used it. But the water also sploshed on the floor by the don't-say-toilet, making it look as if she had pee'd on the lino. So then she had to take some of the soft toilet paper and mop the floor, and then, to dispose of the paper, she had to flush the lavatory again. And if they heard all this, as they well might, or if the housekeeper heard it, her grandmother might later say to her that the lavatory was there for its 'purpose', and not to be played in. Or, worse, that Susan should have attended to her bowels before she left home.

Leaving the lavatory, Susan crept up a brief staircase and went along another corridor, and sidled into what her mother called the book-room.

Susan did not really like these books. She was averse to them. They were fairly uniformly sheathed in uninviting dark skins, and some had gilt lettering, and many were anyway out of her reach. Long ago the old woman had said she might 'look at the books'. Susan had assumed this was exactly what she might do – look. She didn't touch them, except now and then to put her finger on their spines. The titles besides were unencouraging, even unintelligible, like gibberish, and some were in other languages her mother said were French or German, or Latin.

On the long table was a dish. It was of yellowish pale glass, the colour the sherry had been, and it was kept empty.

Susan looked into the dish.

She would have to go back in a moment or be accused of something, having a bowel movement, trespassing, something.

The sun went in beyond the window and sudden rain began to hiss over the thick wild trees which closed the view.

"Susan."

Her mother's voice.

Susan ran from the room, along the corridor, back downstairs, into the passage. Her mother was standing, smoking, in the doorway of the sunken room, and behind her the grandmother stood, not leaning on anything at all, not on a stick, not even the arm of a chair.

"Where have you been?"

"To look at the books."

As if rationally, the grandmother said, "Why don't you stay to lunch, Anne? There's plenty for three."

"No, thank you, Mother. I have to go out this afternoon. I told you. Besides, I left our lunch ready. I can't afford to waste it."

"Let the child stay, then," said the grandmother, hard as granite, demanding a hostage.

"Susan has homework to do."

This was a lie. The one they usually told, when this thing came up about lunch, as so often it did.

"And what," said the grandmother, "will Susan have for lunch in your flat? A sandwich, I suppose."

The mother did not answer. The grandmother stared now, right at the child, "You tell me, then, what is this so-splendid lunch you can't possibly miss?"

Susan looked at her mother, but Anne had turned away.

Hopelessly Susan said, "We're having omelette and chips, Grandmother."

"Ah."

"And tomatoes," apologised Susan.

"Indeed." The grandmother walked across the room. She moved very slowly, stiffly, but without apparent effort. Where was she going? The fireplace? She reached the fireplace, stretched her arm across the mantelpiece, and drew off a small ornament, an apple of rosy china. "Look, do you see? Chipped. That precious woman, who cares for me so well, wantonly chipped it. That's what I think of when I hear the word *chips*. I think of accidents to china, Anne. And so that is what you're giving my grandchild for her lunch. Bits of smashed china ruined by careless servants."

Then she gazed at Susan again. Her eyes were full of – what was it – milk, or venom?

"I shall be taking soup, homemade, of course. Cream of celery, I think. Then a casserole of lamb with dumplings. Roast potatoes and green peas. Then there is some Stilton, but naturally I have raspberry ice-cream, if anyone were to want it."

"Mother, I'm sorry. Perhaps next Sunday –"

"You haven't eaten a meal in this house for ten years."

"That isn't true."

"It is true. What is the point," said the old woman in the pumpkin house, "of my being alive? There you are, the two of you, flesh of my flesh, children of my body, there you are and I am alone. Alone with a petty thief. This is what I have come to."

Or tears. Was that what it was in her eyes? Thick resinous and opaque as glasses fitted *under* the lids. But Susan's grandmother never wore glasses, not even to read. Her eyesight, like her hearing, was still phenomenal.

"Oh for God's sake, Mother." Exasperated, Anne. "Then we must stay. We'll stay for lunch. Yes, very well. Only I wish you'd made this more clear before I'd peeled all those potatoes at home."

"No, no," said the old woman. "No, I can't ask you to stay, I'm afraid. If you'd said before. But there isn't enough for three. Oh, there might be, if that woman didn't squirrel so much of it away for herself. But as it is..."

Somewhere, in another room, a clock struck. One o'clock, or two, who knew, in this limbo of mind-fuck and exasperated despair.

Mrs Danvers, however, re-entered, punctilious as a robot.

"Yes?" asked the grandmother. "Lunch? Already?"

It seemed it was.

"Well, goodbye, Anne. Goodbye, Susan."

They shook themselves, outside, like dogs shaking off the fluids of the vegetable house. They walked for thirty minutes back to the flat in the rain.

"Can we play the card game this afternoon?"

"No. I've got to get ready and go out."

"Oh. Oh –"

"Don't start, Susan."

"You said you'd read through my essay with me."

"I will. Tonight."

"You'll be in late tonight."

"For Christ's sake, stop it."

"Where are you going?"

"Somewhere."

"To the pictures?"

"Perhaps."

"I wish I could go."

"You can. I'll give you the money tomorrow."

"Tomorrow's Monday. It's school."

"Don't talk as if it's spelled H E double L."

"It is."

"I mean, I will take you tomorrow night. If you promise not to make a fuss about getting up on Tuesday morning."

"Will you? Will you? Won't you mind if you've

already seen it?"

"No I won't mind. Eat your chips."

"China chips," said Susan.

"Poor old bitch," said Anne. "God, what can I do?"

"I said we shouldn't go."

"You were quite right."

"Why do we? She hates us. Doesn't want us there, even though she says all that stuff."

"She doesn't hate us. She's very fond of *you*."

"She *isn't*."

"Yes she is. It's just difficult for her to understand. She's a very old lady."

"You said bitch."

"Yes. She is a bitch. So am I. I expect you will be too, when you're older."

Susan, cheered by this inspiring prospect, finished her lunch.

Later, she sat on the edge of the tub as her mother had a bath, admiring Anne's taut curved body, the shallow but beautifully rounded breasts, the fleece of pubic hair, not black or blonde or auburn, but a cool mouse brown.

Then Susan watched her mother paint her toenails, put on a new dress, redo her make-up and spruce up her hair.

"Just made it."

"When will you be back?"

"No later than eleven. Now remember, supper is in the fridge. Don't open the door to anyone, even if they insist they're your fairy-godmother. TV if you like, or that book I've just read was good. It's on my bed, I think. Bye for now."

No information was given, and no question asked about whom she might be going with. Who all the delicious scent and powder and scrupulous time-keeping were for.

A man, Susan did know that. Susan knew about men. Her father had been one, after all, even if she had never seen him. Her mother had only seen him, apparently, one more time than Susan.

When she was younger, Susan hadn't liked being alone so well. Even so, she had *been* alone a lot. Now she didn't mind. Sometimes it made her feel grown-up, the fifteen – or twenty-year-old phase.

She fetched the nail scissors, and began cutting out more thin paper figures.

At nine p.m. the phone went.

Susan answered and gave the number, as people still did then, something which, ten years later, she would never have done. A woman spoke.

"Is that Susan?"

"Yes."

"Can I speak to your mother, please, Susan."

"Mum's out." Should have said Mummy.

"Oh." A long pause. "When will she be back?"

Well drilled in this, as in so much, Susan said, "I'm not quite sure."

"Where is she, do you know?"

"Just at a neighbour's." Also part of the drilling.

The voice sounded relieved. "Oh then, would you mind going along to fetch her for me?"

"I'm not supposed to go out."

"No, but this is urgent. I'm afraid you must. You

won't have to go far if it's just one of the other flats –"

Susan did not know whose the voice was. Presented with the now insuperable dilemma of not revealing that her mother was out until eleven o'clock, (or after) at a location Susan could not be sure of, Susan hesitated.

The voice said, "This is Mrs Marks, Susan. I *need* to speak to your mother *at once*."

Susan did not know what to do, and so she put the receiver down. She had seen her mother respond with this solution quite frequently. When the phone rang again, Susan ignored it, but when it kept on and on ringing it began to make her panicky. She went into the front room and turned up the TV. Finally the phone stopped ringing.

Then it rang every quarter of an hour, rang twenty or thirty times. It began to seem alive, the phone, an enemy.

At five to midnight, when Susan's mother came in, looking tired and drained and lipstickless, the phone had just started to ring again.

"Who on earth is that at this bloody time of night?"

"It's Mrs Danvers."

"*What*?" Anne picked up the phone.

Standing, neurasthenic by now, ears still phone-ringing on and on in the silence, Susan watched her mother's drained face alter, become horribly alert with some invading life-force that had nothing whatever to do with her; heard her say, "When?" Heard her say, "Why?" saw gradually *through* her, as if through a sheet of filmy paper, to some other place beyond that was unidentifiable and yet, peculiarly, also to be recognised.

It was the middle of the night, about two-thirty a.m., when a policeman arrived. After Mrs Danvers, they had gone to bed, and so had to get up again. Anne, confronting the youthful PC, snarled, "I suppose you have to be up all night, so sod us, so do we, is that it?"

"No, madam."

"I thought you always waited twenty-four hours for a disappearance."

"Not always, madam. I understand the lady is very old."

He sat in the front room, asked questions, took some notes. Susan sleepily wandered about making coffee for her mother.

When the policeman had gone, Anne did not return to bed. She paced up and down, smoking cigarettes, frowning.

"Mummy –"

"I'm all right. Go and get some sleep. Bloody woman. Bloody old woman."

They had learned, from Mrs Danvers, that the grandmother had vanished from her lunch table between one fabulous calorific course and the next.

Since this had once or twice happened before, Mrs Danvers hadn't been unduly put out. "She has a habit of coming back, you see, and eating the rest cold."

However, Susan's grandmother did not do that on this occasion. The rich food congealed in its tureens and on its dishes. The half carafe of red wine stood undrunk. "She always has the wine. Her doctor says it's good for her." "I'm sure it is," Anne had said, "it's claret. Ten quid a bottle and that's supposed to be economising, isn't it."

In the afternoon, after the uneaten lunch had been cleared and the service washed, Mrs Danvers put her feet up for a couple of hours, as she generally did, before preparing the five o'clock tea.

"That was when I still couldn't find her," said Mrs Danvers. "At five o'clock."

She then looked, she said, everywhere, and Susan conceived a perhaps-accurate picture of Mrs Danvers patrolling the length and breadth of the abnormal house, up and down all its twisting stairs, along all its tunnels and slopes, in and out of the endless and uncountable rooms. "I even looked up in the attics, Mrs Wilde, and she hasn't been up there for years. The stair is too steep for her, she says."

At nine o'clock Mrs Danvers, concerned and unsure what to do, had called the flat. "But there was a fault on the line, your daughter and I got cut off."

"Yes, quite."

"I kept trying. I couldn't get through."

"No."

"Did I say, I looked all over the garden? I even went through the garden again, in the dark, with a torch."

Standing there in her militant belted mac, like a spy for the Eastern Bloc, Mrs Danvers, who had summoned a taxi to bring her to their door, now announced she had also contacted the police.

"Why?" Anne, (Mrs Wilde) was aghast.

"Well, Mrs Wilde. She hasn't left the house for several years. I think – she's a bit fearful of the outside world. I do all the shopping. I do everything. She never has to go out."

"Obviously then, my mother is still indoors. Mischievously hiding from you. What else would you expect?"

"I hope so, Mrs Wilde."

"Was the cup of coffee all right?" Susan asked, as she was about to leave her mother pacing in the room where the policeman had sat and Mrs Danvers had stood, and where a kind of hollow still remained from their unwanted presences.

"The coffee was disgusting, thank you. Go to bed."

Obscurely frightened, still Susan slept, her body used to the habit of slumber – a handy, childish knack she didn't then suspect might ever desert her.

The next morning, anyway, her grandmother was found.

She had not after all been in the house, or the vast, accumulated garden. She was sitting on a bench in the municipal shrubbery by the Long Pool in the park. There had been a late frost that night, which gathered on her edges, like white crochet. She was completely dead.

"I thought she'd live to be a hundred," said Anne, sombre, speaking softly. "There was nothing wrong with her. Her doctor checked her every three months. He saw her last in January. Her heart was sound. No diseases. She didn't even have rheumatism for Christ's sake. How can she be dead? Oh God, now we've got this death business, forms, mess, and the bloody funeral."

The bloody funeral was actually rather pathetic. She had left, the old woman, explicit instructions for a low-budget burial, at a local cemetery, the plot already purchased. (There was no adjacent grave belonging to anyone. Her husband, Anne's father, had been lost, body and soul, to a Second World War flying bomb in the City.) Anne and Susan attended, and Mrs Danvers in a black coat that was too large and too hot for the tepid rainy afternoon. No one else came.

They stood together over the oblong hole in the earth, and watched the coffin go down, and heard the elderly priest speak about a Christian resurrection that, Anne presently declared, not quite out of earshot, her mother had never believed in.

Afterwards they walked to the nearest pub.

"Of course my daughter is over sixteen," snapped Anne at the barmaid.

In her high heels and eye make-up and lipstick, Susan tried to look worldly and old.

The barmaid let it go; even at sixteen you couldn't supposedly drink alcohol in a pub in those days, and Susan was only having a pineapple juice.

Anne and Mrs Danvers talked desultorarily. Susan ate crisps, wondering incoherently and too lightly what it meant, that hole, that box of darkness and its descent.

She had been aware of the fact of death since she was nine, sitting up one night from sleep, thinking, *One day I'll die.* She never knew what prompted the revelation. She didn't know really if it made her afraid or not. Sometimes, since, she had tried to imagine dying and stopping, or not dying and going on for ever. Both solutions seemed equally alarming and appalling. Gradually the problem faded back in her mind.

Now, she wondered where the old woman, her grandmother, was. If she was anywhere.

"I heard from the solicitors, yes," Mrs Danvers was saying, sipping her magenta vermouth. "She's been generous to me. I did my best, but that's my calling. I certainly didn't expect anything like that."

"The cats' charity will be pleased, too," said Anne, acidly, drinking her second double gin and tonic. "And the other one. What was it? Some medical research or other."

"I'm sure it was an oversight, Mrs Wilde."

"Are you?"

Mrs Danvers seemed uneasy. "It must have been."

"Well if it was, she made a damned good job of it, didn't she. What's the matter with you?" she added to Susan an hour later, as they rode home on the bus.

"I don't know."

"You're not upset, are you?"

"No. I didn't like her. She was awful."

"Yes, she was. I didn't like her, but I'm upset."

"Are you?" Susan stared.

"Because I'm not crying and tearing at my hair doesn't mean I don't feel anything."

Years, twenty years after, Susan would think, That was her mother – *was* she upset? *What* did she feel?

Susan was depressed, and when they got to the flat, the grey wet warm light trapped inside, depressed her further.

She understood, from what her mother had told her, that the grandmother had left all her money, except for the mediocre funeral expenses, and several thousands of pounds for Mrs Danvers-known-as-Marks, to various charities. Even the house had been left to a charity devoted to the succour of cats. "I didn't know she liked cats," Mrs Danvers had remarked, defensively bemused. "She never had a cat. A shame really. I'm quite fond of them myself. I'd have had one, if I'd known."

Anne had been left nothing. Not even a keepsake. Nor, as far as Susan knew, had Anne taken anything for herself from the house. But who would want any of those heavy and dismaying things, the non-edibly chipped pieces of china, the cumbersome Victorian furniture, none of it, even so, properly antique or of any beauty. Anything of value was itemised and to be sold. Had there been jewellery? Susan saw none.

"Did you ever live here when you were little?" Susan had once asked Anne, years before the disappearance, the park bench, and death. "No. I lived with my aunt in Lincoln. I've told you." "Oh, yes." Estranged, always separate. Strangers going by the misnomer of Relation.

"I don't want to go to school tomorrow," said Susan.

"You never want to."

Susan hung her head.

"All right, all right. It's Friday anyway. Have a long weekend."

A weight hung about Susan's neck through Friday, alone in the flat, while her mother worked. And also through Saturday. Like the Albatross, or one of the walnut mammoths of furniture from the vegetable house.

On Saturday night Anne went out with a man.

Susan mooched about the rooms, unable to sustain

an interest in anything. She put all the lights on, too.

"Why are all the lights on?" said Anne when she came home at one a.m. "I've said, don't do that, Susan. I have to spend enough on bills as it is."

"A light bulb only costs a penny for three hours. I read it somewhere."

"Rubbish."

The next day was Sunday. Sunday, the day of visits to the old woman.

There had already been two Sundays after her death, of course. But they were taken up with seeing to things to do with the funeral, or the clearing of the house.

What had she died of, the grandmother?

"Old age."

"It says heart failure on the form."

"That's what everyone dies of. It was old age."

But Susan thought of the words *heart failure*. A lapse of the heart, not only unable anymore to beat, but to reason, to reply, to communicate – This heart was a failure.

Between Saturday night and Sunday, Susan dreamed of her grandmother, which surely she had never done before.

Somewhere she must have seen a photograph of her. Perhaps even somewhere in the vegetable house, though she couldn't recall this, before or while it was eviscerated and cleared. This certainly was how Susan's grandmother appeared in the dream, in a photographic sepia tone, and young.

What she was doing, under her light-coloured, piled-up hair, Susan never noticed. Maybe nothing.

Maybe she just stood there, young and slender, half-smiling, wide-lambent-eyed.

"Who's that? It's Catherine."

In the dream all the name took on meaning for Susan, for she had seen it on a marriage certificate among dusty black boxes of things, as her mother swore and wrestled with the eldritch furniture.

"Was this her?"

"What? Yes, yes, that was her. And that was my father. Richard Arlen John Wilde. They were married in 1907."

"It says. But that's her own name."

"That was her maiden name. It's an odd name, isn't it? She used to be proud of it."

So the old woman's name was not Grandmother, or Susan's Grandmother, or even Anne's mother.

Catherine Greyglass, that had been her name. How strange indeed, for had that been what Susan had been seeing all the time in her eyes, only that, glass – grey glass?

II

The summer, four years later, was incredible. Glowing day followed day, under skies of thick stretched blue light. It felt like Italy, or, when the dusty-spicy sunsets came, the edge of Africa in a film.

In late August, one evening, walking home, and seeing the running honey sunshine reflected high up in the trees of the common, Susan felt that something, not just summer, was coming to an end. And it was.

"What's for dinner, Anne?" (Mum and Mummy – both were gone more than a year. "I want to call you Anne." And, to Anne's flawless, raised eyebrows, "You're a person, not just my mother." Irrefutable compliment. "Yes, all right," said Anne, and became Anne. Because you couldn't keep on saying Mummy, after you were fifteen.)

"Dinner? Hyena on toast."

But it was salad. Anne had, for about eighteen months, been leaving her book-keeping job in central London at three-thirty, to beat the rush hour. "I'm indispensable, I've got another raise, too. No one can add up nowadays. Not even you." This was true enough. Susan was sometimes impressively literate, but nearly innumerate, and had failed maths without a backward glance.

"You don't want to go back this new term, do you?" Anne had said.

"No."

"Do you want to try Silverguilds?"

They had looked at each other. When Susan didn't reply, Anne said, "Art college is fine, Susan. Your Miss Whatsit said Silverguilds would certainly take you, and you could get a grant."

Susan shrugged. She was secretly afraid, at sixteen, of the enormous adult world she had always, until recently, hankered after. Its seeming freedoms having gradually, by her own observation, been revealed to her as slavery, a condition of grim responsibility and personal onus childhood had not equipped her for. And she must Work, have a Job. But what? For Susan, she existed. That was the Job. But it wasn't enough. You had to earn money and take your Place. And surely she was fairly ungifted? You can speak French, they said. It could be got to a higher standard, and you could teach. (This thought was withering.) Susan began to stammer whenever she spoke French in class. Otherwise the art mistress, a long, pear-shaped woman with a wet nose, told Susan she might make a career in commercial art, and so the phantom of Silverguilds had swum into sight. "I won't get in," Susan said. Even if she did, art college was just another kind of school. The child's, if not the adult's slavery, would go on. Getting up at the crack of dawn in winter, told what to do, given homework, bored, frustrated. Not inarticulate, yet she did not say, could not sort it out to say, only look sullen. Would not enthuse. True to form, Anne ignored her. By August there had been a successful interview, the grant promised, everything settled.

When the salad was eaten, Susan made coffee. They

went on to the balcony to drink it, for this was not the flat of four years previously. Six weeks after the old woman died, they had moved nearer to inner London, and a couple of years after that, moved again, here, an upmarket, three-roomed apartment, with clean white walls and a view.

It was Friday, and Susan knew Anne was going out again tonight. Then Anne surprised her by saying, "What will you do this evening?"

"Oh, I'll play records."

"Or," Anne paused, "why don't you come with me?"

"But you're going out."

"Yes."

Susan looked at Anne. "But you're going out with a man."

"*Yes*. And the same one I've been seeing for quite a long time."

"Oh good." Embarrassed, accustomed to total exclusion in this quarter, and happy by now with that, Susan felt a prickly unease creep through her body. "So..."

"So, why not come and meet him."

This was unheard of. Unheard of for anyone. One's mother's boyfriend.

"Why?" said Susan. She felt frightened. She often did, now. The fright was never coherent, yet vaguely everywhere, lurking.

"Why not?"

"No thanks."

"All right." Anne gazed across at the trees of the common, divided from them only by the wide and noisy, fuming main road, the ashes of the day. "But you'll be meeting him anyway, Susan. He's coming to lunch tomorrow."

"Well, I can go out. Jo and I were going to look for some shoes –"

"No, I don't want you to go out. I want you to stay in. Doll yourself up and make yourself a pretty girl, and meet Wizz."

Susan's mouth opened. A laugh leapt fluttering and cackling out like a demented hen.

"Yes, it's a funny name isn't it. A nickname. Glad you like it. He calls us Wizz and Wilde, the Unbeatable Duo. Alliteration, the thing you like such a lot."

Anne, at nearly forty-six, still kept her pure, scarcely-lined skin, was svelte and glamorous. Her hair was nowadays a shoulder-length, lustrous copper. On her good days, which were many, she looked forty or less. Only first thing in the morning, sometimes last thing at night, did she seem her age, or any real age at all.

But Susan had still not become herself, and intuitively knew it. She was not pretty. Heavy, and inclined to acne, she hid in her own long fair hair, like a pig in grass. She hated, of course, to be inspected. Preferred to forget her outer case, waiting, in the hope of miraculous change, some science fiction invention that might save her.

She had never, herself, essayed a boyfriend. No one had been 'interested'. She had had 'crushes' on unattainable beings glimpsed on buses and trains, in films and on TV.

Her mother was quite another animal, and lived in

another world.

"I can't make myself *pretty*."

"Yes you can. Wear your blue dress."

"I spilled something on it."

"Oh for God's sake. I'm not asking you, I'm telling you, Susan. Listen to me. Things have become serious, between Wizz and me."

"Wizz –"

"Yes, Wizz. *Wizz*. His real name is Derek. He prefers Wizz. Wouldn't you?"

"No."

"You have to meet him."

"Why? He's yours not mine."

"You're jealous?"

"Of course I'm not –" Incestuously affronted, Susan felt her face go scarlet.

"Listen, Susan. No more arguments. You're going to meet him. It's important."

"*Why*?"

"I'm going to live with him, you stupid child. Are you really so dumb? And there is a chance – a wonderful chance – we may be going to America."

"Wh – "

"Yes, the States. Now what do you say?"

Told to open the door, Susan stood behind it for as long as she could. Then of course he rang again. So she opened it wide and tried to smile confidently and in the correct hostess manner. But the smile stuck, keeping her face pulled open in a rictus, like the door. Wizz had amazed her.

"You must be Sue."

"Yes, I'm Susan."

"Hi, Sue."

He was not American. From the little Anne had said, Susan had half expected him to be. But he had a strong East London accent. That was a surprise too.

Over the years, very, very occasionally, Susan had caught odd glimpses of the men her mother was dating. They were seen from the front room window, for example, walking Anne home from the bus-stop, or pulling up in a car. Once even, one arrived at the flat when Anne was out with someone else. No one was 'serious', but they were all quite presentable, two had even been handsome.

But Wizz looked like a film star.

"Can I come in?" Wizz asked, with arch enquiry.

She let him through, and straggled after him, and saw him go straight into the living room and plaster himself straight up against Anne. The x-certificate kiss left both Anne and Susan speechless.

"What do you think?" said Anne, that night, when they were alone again. This too was arch – or nervous?

"He's very good-looking."

"Yes. He's nine years younger than me. Oh, he knows. What's nine years? And his clothes are so good. Even his casual wear is smart. He can afford a tailor."

"What does he do?"

"Oh, this and that. He's with a firm of importers."

As one would expect from a film star, Wizz's teeth blazed white in a mahogany tan. His dark hair had that thick combed lushness. His long narrow eyes were clear, and of a pale arctic blue. His manicured hands were horrible, vulgar, hairy, with thick sausage fingers, one looking lethally constricted by its gold ring.

His voice got louder during lunch, too, as they drank the wine he had brought. He smoked, and mashed out his fags, Chesterfields, on the plate.

He acted like a boy. "What's for pudding, Mummy?" he asked Anne. He said, innocently, of the flowers he had also brought, "Who gave you all those flowers?" Susan hated the stodgy expression 'pudding'. Where had he picked it up? Why did he need re-thanking for the flowers? He spoke more or less grammatically, but his loud voice mangled the words. Sometimes he donned a fake American accent, like a DJ. He sprawled in the chair, spreading, his lunched waist bulging now he had undone his jacket. He smelled of expensive aftershave and something else.

He boasted.

"This guy, right, I'm telling you, we had nothing but trouble with this geezer. So I goes to him, Hey man, I said, Are you going to stop mucking us around or what? And this guy, you're not going to believe this – this guy says, It's the delivery boys. I said, And I've got fairies at the bottom of my arse."

Anne was tight from the wine. Wizz was either tight or drunk. Shut out from this camaraderie of the pissed, as she was from their sexual union, Susan felt older than either of them, impatient and annoyed. And petrified, scared of what they might do next.

When she sobered up, Anne would realise this man was awful. Evidently, he could never have behaved like this before.

But no, he must have. She thought he was all right.

"Okay, ma'am," said Wizz in a Texan accent. And Anne laughed.

He made little conversation with Susan. He flashed her white smiles, (toothpicked pristine at the table) and expected, with a touching self-confidence, that Susan must like him. But within half an hour even his extreme looks were turning like eggs. The teeth, so displayed, were too long. His eyes too small. He was too – *there*.

Wizz changed things. He never addressed Anne as Anne. When not calling her ma'am or Mummy, he called her Wilde. "Wizz and Wilde," he said to Susan. "the Unbeatable Duo." Susan he called, Sue, Suky, Sue-Ellen and once, Suey Fuey.

"Here, I've got to go over there next week. Might have a couple of spare tickets." He was speaking now of the U.S.A.

Susan felt sick with terror. She had only felt startled before.

He saw her face and said, "Never been up in a plane? Flying – nothing to it. Sometimes I do it four, five times a month."

"I'm supposed to start at college," said Susan.

"College'll keep."

Susan offered to wash up. They let her. As she was running the water, she heard Wizz murmuring and then Anne said, laughing, "No, not now, Wizz." "We'll go in your room. She's not a kid. She knows the score, don't she?" "Not here." "Send her out. Send her to buy something. What haven't you got?"

Later, when Anne was in the bathroom, he came into the kitchen, which was small, and so he seemed to take up all the space. He looked into cupboards, picked things up and put them down.

"Well," he said, "what d'ya think?"

"Sorry?"

"About The Trip?" It had two capital T's.

Susan mumbled something, trying to placate him. She was afraid they would accidentally touch if he didn't soon leave the kitchen. His smell was overpowering, aftershave and booze and, somehow, some sort of bad smell she couldn't identify, for he was immaculate.

Afterwards, she could not, must not say to Anne, "He smelled funny." Anne was fastidious and choosy. And she liked him. She slept with him, even if she wouldn't do it in the flat when Susan was there. So… it must be Susan's imagination, the faint stench.

When she had finished the washing up, Susan had to go back to the balcony, where they were both now sitting in the sun.

"How about I take both my girls for a ride?"

Wizz was including Susan, trying to make her adult and important, attractive, valuable enough to be a possession: my girls. Susan smiled wanly. "You go. It's all right." As if tactfully giving up a treat so the lovers could let rip.

She thought Anne would argue, insist. But Anne only laughed. So they went. From the window, Susan saw Anne and Wizz (Wizz and Wilde) drive off the flat forecourt in his big, expensive, gleaming car. It was three o'clock. Anne came back at midnight, alone. "That car is so comfortable. That's the fifth car he's had since I've known him. He's always changing them."

"What does his firm import?" Susan asked in desperation; obviously they had to talk on and on about Wizz.

"*I* don't know. Everything, I think."

"How did you meet?" Trying to be interested, to please Anne.

"Oh that." Anne, taking off with cold cream her cosmetics, what Wizz had left of them, paused. "He came into the office. There was some kind of palaver about something. I wasn't really listening. Mr V got in his usual flap. Then... *he* came and leaned over my desk."

In the stories Wizz had told, stories which never seemed to have a beginning or any real ending, the other characters were always making excuses, crawling – in a flap, like Mr V.

"What did he say? Did he just ask you out?"

"He just said, Are you free for dinner tonight? I said, No, I can't. He said, Tomorrow then. I said, Yes."

The flat had smelled on and on of Wizz after he left, despite the summer-wide windows. A stagnant odour, like old plant water.

They had had cocktails, apparently, at the Waldorf. And probably, Susan thought, gone up to a bedroom.

"I'll write to Silverguilds. You can start the course a week or so late. It won't hurt."

"No, I don't want to go."

"Don't be silly. Not *go* – to the States! I haven't been abroad since I was in my twenties. Never America. I can't wait. Of course we'll go. Thank God I got the passport situation sorted out last month. There, you see, you've even got a passport. That's a thrill isn't it?"

"I don't –"

"Air travel is nothing. It's easy. They won't expect us to fly the plane ourselves."

"It's just –"

"Susan, listen to me. Soon he may be going to live over there. Indefinitely. And he wants me to live with him, and I want to, Susan. Oh God, do I. I'd get shot of this flat. No rent to find. He'd see to visas, everything."

Susan felt her carefully knit expression cracking into sections, which slipped from her and lay along the floor.

"Don't pull that face. What's the matter with you? It's a glorious, wonderful chance. Christ, Susan, what's here that's so special? Silverguilds? You've never shown much enthusiasm." Susan found to her own shock that she started to cry. "Stop it. *Stop* it, Susan. I don't want to spend the rest of my bloody days in this dump, breathing in car fumes, working in some hole-in-the-corner job. I want to see some action." A phrase Wizz might have used? "New York – oh, Susan, you can't begin to see, can you, it will be so exciting. Any other girl, she'd be crazy to go."

"He's weird," Susan blurted. "I think he's a crook – a gangster –"

"Oh don't be so ridiculously melodramatic and –"

"All those men he told us about, saying sorry, sorry, and blaming other people – and he smells."

Anne's face reached a crescendo of rage and burst, unexpectedly – to both of them, it seemed – in a torrent of helpless mirth.

"*Smells*? You're mad, child. Smells of money, yes. Of life. Go to bed for fuck's sake."

And so they parted for the night, Anne laughing, Susan crying.

In the morning, as usual in the holidays, Anne left for work before Susan woke. Anne had pinned a note on the corkboard in the kitchen, but all it said was, *Please get another pint of milk and a large Hovis. Merci.*

Susan showered and dressed rebelliously. She made up rebelliously, painting out her spots by the accustomed method, using a paintbrush and disc of white eye make-up, then applying layers of powder and blusher. Jo had once told Susan she put shadow on her lids like a panda. Anne, though, her mother, never made a criticism like this.

"It won't happen," Susan said to the painted face in the mirror, (make it laugh at that.)

After she had gone out and bought the milk and bread, and a pound of plums, Susan checked her funds. There seemed quite a lot of money saved from her allowance.

When she thought of the Trip, which constantly she did, Susan felt sick. When she thought of Wizz she felt sick.

The flat throbbed with induced nausea.

All that summer break she had been roaming about with Jo, her half-friend from school, a looming, argumentative, ungainly girl who wore glasses. Susan was tired of Jo by now, and anyway, it would only take one long bus-ride to conduct her back in time, to the land before Wizz and America.

When she turned into Constance Street, the aura of its

familiarity was sharp, almost surreal. Dazed, Susan gaped at the old houses and the tall dusty trees, so well remembered, the garish off-licence on the corner, the Chinese take-away, the post-office. Here it all was, still intact, the past. But then she came to the wall of the house where she had lived with Anne, and the wall was there but the house was not.

Susan stood in the open gateway, staring up a tarmac drive parked over with cars, to a five-storey modern block of flats. On either side, the other houses rose aloof, entire. Only her own building, hers and Anne's, had been eradicated. It was like a plot against them, to expunge their image, pretend they had never been, and if they said they had – they *lied*.

A woman flounced out of the flats. She wore a white suit and a lot of gold jewellery. She unlocked a bright red car, got in, and presently drove out right past Susan, still standing gawping in the widened gap in the wall, where once a gate had been.

Susan walked along the street. She stared up into the burnt green clusters of the chestnut trees. Everything was there, just the same, except for the house where she and Anne had lived.

Turning into Dunkirk Street though, Susan found some trees had been planted along the pavements in wire cages. Someone had white graffitoed over the Dun of Dunkirk and written in above, *Capt*.

Susan walked, not knowing whether to turn back, to see if her own building had reappeared. But that was silly. So she kept walking, and Capt. Kirk Street led, sooner than she recalled, into the park. Susan bought an ice-cream, from a van in the park, with a chocolate stick stuck in it. This was to compensate for the demolishment of her roots, and also for all the times she had been dragged through the park and not allowed to stop.

The park still looked big, but swept bare. Had it always been so bleak, even in summer? Long blank vistas of lawn, the groups of trees standing well back to the sides, as if unwilling to ask each other to dance. Among the trees in the left hand areas were the public toilets, and beyond, the path which led to the shrubbery and the Long Pool.

Susan finished the ice-cream, even the less-appetising cornet. Then she walked through the park and straight into Tower Road.

"I don't want to go up there," she had said. And Anne had always made her.

I don't want to go to America and live with Wizz.

Could Anne make her do that too?

Tower Road, the prehistoric riverbed, roped its way among the cliffs of mossy, tree-hung walls, the cascades of foliage. It was midday, the sun directly overhead and raw with fire. Grasshoppers scratched among the hot stones. There was the antique sound of water, hidden behind brickwork, trickling, and in the blue-black recurring shade, a visual silence.

Why go on? No one was making her, now. There was no reason. The reason had been found on a bench, in a crochet of white frost, four years ago, dead.

"Hello – are you Helen Cully?"

"No."

"No, I thought you weren't. I think she's older. And

delayed, obviously. But it's okay anyway, if you want to come in. The more the merrier."

They walked up the drive.

The thing that struck Susan first, when the door was open, was the excruciating reek of cats' urine. It was like a blow, so she grunted involuntarily and put her hand over her mouth, then took it down, because that would be rude.

"Yes, sorry about the pong," said the woman, unconcerned. "We do our best, but we've got around two hundred on our hands now, and a lot of them aren't litter trained as yet, or neutered. It's the males spraying that's the worst."

She was about thirty-five, slim and boyish in her jeans and T–shirt, with spiky brunette hair, a clear sandy complexion and aquamarine eyes.

The stink, and the sight of several black and white cats among the bushes outside, now augmented by three tabbies cantering almost in tandem across the wide hall like a chariot team, provided recollection.

"Oh, the cats' charity."

"That's us. Cat Samaritans. I thought that was why you were here, to have a look and choose one – or preferably six or seven of the buggers. Aren't you?"

"Sorry."

They stood in the hall. Meows sang through the upper air.

Aside from the cats, it was not as she remembered, not really. It seemed more empty, lighter. Bars of sun fell dramatically across the floor, which had new lino of a cold beige. Some of the trees had been cut back, by the walls, that was it, allowing the sunshine to pass in.

The drive, though, had been if anything more overgrown, all but a central strip where the wheels of jeeps had recently smashed through the weeds.

The house itself, seen from the outside, as Susan had stood there on the driveway – the house… Somehow she had kept looking and looking at it, trying to see it, for somehow it wasn't there, just like the flats in Constance Street. Somehow, the house had vanished.

And yet – they had just walked through the door. They were inside the house.

The woman, who had come around the non-house and advanced toward her, mistaking her for the delayed Helen Colly, now said, "Oh come and have a cup of tea anyway. If you can stand the smell."

"It's all right, really. I like cats."

"Yes," said the woman. "I like cats better than people, frankly. There's five of us here at the moment, on the team. But I'm the only real peoplephobe."

"I'm people… " said Susan inanely.

"Oh, you're all right. You're a cat really," said the woman, strangely. "I'm Jackie, by the way."

"Susan. My grandmother used to live here."

They were in the kitchen by then, the lower kitchen right at the back of all the sunken regions of the house. They had waded there through waves of cats, which came rushing, screaming, towards them. Every one had a name, by which Jackie greeted them. Some had only three legs, or one eye, but all looked spruce, well-fed and healthy. Snake-like, they rubbed their soft fur over the women's legs. And when Susan sat down at the long wooden table, two jumped as one into her lap.

"Just put them off if they bother you."

"No... they're great."

"Let me get this straight. Your grandmother was Mrs Wilde —"

"Mrs Catherine Wilde." Susan smoothed the cats, which slapped her under the chin with their tails, trampling her knees down to the proper consistency. Then she smoothed the kitchen table. It was the library table. That was where she had seen it last. In the book-room with the pale jaundiced dish on it, reflecting back her own round, half-formed, twelve-year-old face.

"She left us the house," said Jackie, "as you know. It was an absolute godsend, I can tell you. We were trying to do this out of two basement flats."

The lap-cats settled, edges and tails overlapping.

The rest of the tidal sea of fur ceaselessly moved back and forth through the kitchen, reminding Susan of the Countess Gertrude in *Gormenghast*. All the dim chambers of the house rang with meowing, purrs, snarls and screeches, sudden skitterings and thumps.

"I remember that plant. I used to call it Martian Rhubarb. It's got much bigger."

"Yeah, there were a lot of plants left. We take cuttings and start new ones, sell them when we have a jumble sale for the cats."

Another woman stalked into the kitchen, older, with long grey hair and a cross face.

"Do you know where the tablets are for the Putney Six?"

"Try behind the rag-cupboard like last time."

"That window needs fixing again upstairs. And that

knocking's started again."

She marched out. Susan drank some of the tea Jackie had put before her. She was becoming used to the urine-reek, noticing it less or not at all.

"Must seem strange to you. Us being here now."

"Yes."

"I gather she was quite a character, the old lady."

Susan didn't know what to say.

The strawberry-red leaves of the Martian Rhubarb, either the original, or a cutting, and now a massive three-foot high in a plastic tub, stirred suddenly, whispered to each other, rasped like dry old skin.

Jackie glanced at the plant.

"Did you want to look around the house?"

"Oh – maybe."

"Go ahead, if you want."

"Oh, but –"

"Frankly, Susan, I trust you. And even if you were a thief, we haven't got much to steal, apart from the cats. And providing you can prove you have a good home for them you can have as many of those as you want, free."

"Wish I could," said Susan, politely.

She didn't know if she wanted to go over the house. She had never, so far as she could recall, even come this distance, in her grandmother's day, never seen the lower kitchen or the scullery. But now she supposed she must, must look at the house. It was full of an ocean of cats. No longer as it had been. No longer – *here*.

As she flexed her legs, wondering how to remove the two sleepers without jolting them, both woke and instantly sprang from her, indifferent to the passage of humans and random fate.

Was this a bit like having to go round a stately home on a school visit, something she had to do, and pretend to be interested in? How many rooms *were* there? They had been added on decades before, the house – already large – extending in all directions. Some rooms even no longer had windows, being trapped between outer rooms which did, or so Anne had once said. Susan found none of these. But Anne hadn't seen much of the house, had never lived, *consciously* in the house. The grandmother, Catherine, had conceived Anne unexpectedly in her late forties. And then World War II had happened, and Anne, only about four or five, was sent to a well-to-do aunt, (her father's sister) on a farm outside Lincoln. She never came back.

But really, Susan knew nothing about all that, as Anne seemed not to. Susan knew nothing about her – about Catherine. Nothing.

Of the cats, with which the house was now mainly furnished, Susan met all kinds, even a pair of Persians on a landing, who stared at her with demented apricot eyes.

Once she saw another human, a thin hurrying girl in trousers, who simply muttered "Hi" and trotted past.

A few doors were shut, and Susan left them alone. In some open-doored rooms were large cages, with single cats in them, presumably segregated due to ailments or unsocial temperament.

But the house – room on room, corridor on corridor, steps, annexes, was, despite cats and absence, still a vegetable house, a pumpkin: the Labyrinth.

Then somehow, coming down a crooked back stair, Susan emerged into a wide room empty of all furniture. Trees pressed at the windows, fir, pines, bays, and beyond lay an unexpected growing wall of garden, turning back from a once-pruning into a jungle.

This was the room, still cased in its emerald light, where Susan and Anne had last seen the old woman alive.

Cats lay in patches of sun on bare boards. Marks of territorial cat sprayings decorated the plaster, to an impressively high point.

But it was still *that* room.

Susan stood there.

She had thought she was lost in the house, had even uneasily wondered if she could find her way down to the front again, and if not would she be unable ever to get out?

But here she was.

The room was full of an immense stillness. Nothing moved that made any sound, not even the cats. Before a window, standing on the floor, another Martian Rhubarb, darker and greener than the other, raised its heavy flags to the scattered sun.

One by one the cats lifted their eyes, some their heads, looking all one way, towards a vacant spot in the room where a shaft of light faded slowly, perhaps unaccountably. The cats watched. They looked steadily up into the air, where nothing was, and followed it with their gem stone eyes.

Fine hairs rose on the back of Susan's neck.

After a moment, the light changed again. A cloud must have crossed the sun. The cats resumed former occupations, mostly sleeping. Two began to fight. One bounded into the pot of the plant and urinated.

Jackie was standing talking in a room off the hall, with a big woman in a Laura Ashley dress. "Oh, yes, I'd like to adopt three, even four." Helen Colly? That was all right then.

Near the front door, the grey-haired woman bent over a hamper with kittens in it.

"Thanks for calling," she said to Susan, harshly. "Thinking of joining the team? It's a tough life, you know. We'll be out again tonight, all night, I expect, trying to catch ferals and bring them in. And every cat needs to be thoroughly checked over, you know, neutered, some need drugs. Look at these, abandoned in Hawthorne Road."

"Poor things," said Susan. She gazed at their milky grey eyes.

"Oh, they'll be all right now. But it costs a lot. We do like a donation, where possible."

Flushing, feeling like a criminal, Susan rummaged for a pound note and gave it to the woman. She imagined over and over, as she walked back up the drive, the woman saying to her colleagues, "Flash little bitch, handing me a pound like some duchess." Or, alternatively saying, "Mean little cow. Only gave me a quid."

"Had an okay day?"

"Mr V had one of his famous attacks," said Anne, scathingly. "I get the feeling they're going to fold the business up."

Susan turned her head from the rescuing spectres of Wizz and America the Golden, glinting at the back of her mother's silver eyes.

"Anne – tell me about Grandmother."

"What? What am I supposed to tell you, after all these years?" Anne flopped gracefully back in her chair, drinking icy orange-juice from the fridge, shoes kicked off, her feet, with their perfectly enamelled nails, propped on the stool. Heat lay over the flat like damp washing. "I'm tired, Susan. I'm going to have another bath. The trains are bloody in this weather –"

"I'll run the bath for you."

"Thanks."

When Susan came back, she said, "Do you remember anything about the house, Anne?"

"Which house?"

"The house in Tower Road. When you were little and lived there with Grand – with Catherine."

"No."

"Not even –"

"I've said, You've asked me before and I've told you all I know. I remember being about four, and saying, Am I four? And someone said Yes. That may have been my father, or her. I don't recollect. And I don't remember anything about the house, it was just a sort of space around things. I don't even remember the garden, except a piece with roses growing up something. That's all. I'm not putting you off, Susan. I truly don't remember a thing."

"But you remember the farm. The drive with the lilacs. And Lincoln. How it was so flat, except for the hill with the castle and the cathedral. And the Roman arch in that street. All that."

"Oh yes. But I was there until I was in my twenties."

"I went there today."

"Lincoln?" Anne looked quizzical, waiting.

"The house. Her house."

"My God. What sort of state was it in?"

Susan smiled. "It was full of cats."

"Yes, it would be."

"No, it was nice. They take care of them and find them proper homes and everything."

"How much did you give them?"

"Only a pound."

"That's quite a lot at your age, on our income."

"But they let me look round. I'd never seen so much of the house, and it's so peculiar, and I couldn't make any – sense of it –"

"No," said Anne. "They kept building on. It was a shambles. They were both mad, you know. Richard and Catherine. And then he got killed in London, when that bomb landed in the street. And that just left her to be mad on her own."

"Did she want you back then?"

"No, she never wanted me at all. They didn't want children, and she thought she'd never have any. And then, there I was. She was forty-seven, forty-eight. A horrible difficult birth. They had to sew her up. She told me once."

"Oh – ugh –"

"You asked. So listen. I think she'd have given me away whatever happened, the War just provided a decent excuse. Before my late twenties, I saw her only once, when I was twenty-one. She came to my party. I didn't know who she was. Aunt Margaret said, Here's your mother, Anne. Can you picture it?"

"What did she look like?"

"Old. I was twenty-one, and she was – what would she have been – about sixty-seven or eight – nearly seventy. She had on a cream costume, and her hair was still fair, or she'd had it dyed, and it was permed in the latest fashion. Blood-red nails and lips. This was in the Fifties. Women looked like that then. But not necessarily old ones. She gave me a present. Oh, I'd had things before. They came by post. She *handed* me this."

"What was it?"

"It was a cheque for a hundred pounds. That was real money then. Go and turn the bath off before it runs over."

Susan went, shut off the taps, darted back. But now Anne looked at her moodily. "Look, Susan. I don't really want to talk about this now. I didn't know her, and suddenly she expected to be my mother. Margaret wasn't exactly peerless, but she did her best. She was the closest I got. And then this dolled-up praying mantis appears before me."

"You said –"

"I've said enough. Shut up. I'm going to have that bath. Oh," pausing in the doorway, deliberate and cruel with her ace card, "thought any more about America?"

The phone rang when Anne was in the bathroom.

It was Jo.

"I tried you all afternoon," accusingly. "Where were you?"

"I went out."

"Can you come for a walk? I want to ask you something."

"Maybe. I'll see. What?"

"Tell you then. Meet you by Stratfords."

Jo was already waiting by the shop, looking carefully at an array of oil-heaters, kitchen implements, and crockery in the window. Her tall sausage-like body was clad in a longish skirt and loose blouse. Her short, naturally-blonde hair, her only potential attraction, was greasy and pushed back behind big ears, as if she meant deliberately to be as charmless as she was able.

Susan could not be proud of Jo. Could not introduce her to anyone with a flood of pride – "My friend, Jo." She resented this in Jo, and felt guilty for resenting it. It didn't matter what people looked like. (No?) On the other hand, Jo could also be tactless, critical, and sometimes something that Susan would later refer to, in her late twenties, as *spiritually obtuse*.

They walked along the public paths of the common, as the last russet light dripped through the trees.

Young men, bare bronze-armed and legged, strode or bicycled past them, casting neither of them a single glance.

Nor did Jo have a boyfriend. She appeared not to want one. She was going to secretarial school, and an uncle had already promised her a lucrative secure job in a big London office. This seemed to be her only goal. Jo had never been in love, not even with anyone on celluloid. "Oh him," she would say. "He's all right, I suppose." Even when Susan spoke admiringly of some glamorous woman: "Wish I could look like that," Jo would sniff, "They don't look like that in real life, you know." How did Jo know anyway? Jo was very good at maths.

"My dad says I can have a flat," said Jo abruptly. "I mean, when I start college. It would mean I was nearer to college, and save time in the long run."

"Really? A flat?"

"Well, a room. But a good one in a respectable house. Clean. No people taking drugs, fixing."

"You *are* lucky." Susan did not know if she really thought this, but clearly congratulations and envy were expected. "Are you pleased?"

"Well, I will be. But the only thing is, Dad says I have to share with another girl. He says it's not safe, me being there on my own. And if I shared, the expenses would be halved, of course."

"Yes."

"So, what do you think?"

Susan stared at Jo. "Me?"

"Dad says you're steady. He likes your Mum – the Brave and Fair Anne, he calls her," she added, too thick to be ashamed of him. "He said I should ask you. It would be handy for Silverguilds, too, because that's near my secretarial college. We could travel on the same bus. And you'll have your grant, same as I will, and there'll be what Dad gives me, too."

Susan thought about sharing a room with Jo. The prospect was rather unappealing. Jo was a stickler for all sorts of things – she liked rules, (knowing where she stood, as Jo put it.) She liked lots of little ornaments, and dusting them…

"Only," Susan said, "my mother – we may be going to the U.S.A."

"For a holiday?"

"Sort of. It's a bit more than that."

Jo's unemotive face settled. "All right then. I'll have to ask someone else."

"Jo – I don't want to go to the States – I'd hate it – she's got this horrible man – he's foul –"

Jo stared at Susan with a deep latent intriguement striving behind the dough of her cheeks. "Why?"

"He just is. I want to stay here."

"Shall I speak to your mum," said the deadly grown-up Jo, "about my flat?"

"No. I'll talk to her. Tomorrow."

"All right. But I need to know soon. I'm already having to start college from home, and that's going to cost a lot and be a long journey."

America seemed familiar because of TV. There were the same terracotta and brown brownstones, baking in hot, late summer light, the same sidewalks, playgrounds and lots, and, at the centre of the city of New York, the same incredible surrounding image of a metropolis of the far future coexisting here and now.

Coming in over the highways and bridges, darkness already down on the September air, (which smelled of cinders and gasoline) the lighted skyscrapers rose from the void, pinned by a million diamonds to the night. And then later, other floodlit buildings lifted twenty miles above the ends of Manhattan's cobbles, like waterfalls of blue ice with ruby spires.

But wonder was prevented from spreading its

wings. Because Wizz was there, in the car, and the aura of Wizz overlaid everything.

"What d'ya think?" he asked them, driving boldly on the 'wrong' side of the road in yet another vast flash car. As if he had invented the city, or *discovered* it, like a sort of belated Columbus. Did they have to thank him for building New York?

Downtown, Upstate, said the signs slung above the road.

They drove into Manhattan, to Wizz's loft.

After all, Anne and Susan hadn't flown to the States with Wizz, he had only picked them up at Kennedy International (JFK, said Wizz.)

At Heathrow, Anne took Susan straight into a bar. "Let's pretend you're eighteen, Susan. Then you can have a gin and tonic with me." This by now sometimes happened at home. And Susan was so nervous she had been more than glad of the dizzy quick glow the gin gave her. By the time they walked down the claustrophobic area, (screened as if from horrors) on to the plane, everything seemed feasible, and all right.

The flight was uneventful, enervating due to the cramped seats. Wizz's tickets had put them in Business Class, but Anne had seemed a little disappointed. At one time she had been speaking predictively of Concorde.

Sometimes, beyond the window, Susan saw clouds below her, wrapped over the blue surface of the world, as if she watched the earth from space. Coupled with the glass of wine she had had with the plane meal, this too seemed to put everything in perspective. The in-flight film was oddly dreamlike; she dozed. When she came to, they were nearly there. Susan now felt warm and sleepy and dirty. Apprehensive. Anne though was all alight, make-up redone, hair burnished, only the lines rather too deep at the sides of her eyes and mouth. "Wizz! Wizz darling!" she exclaimed, as they emerged from immigration – where arrest had seemed, to Susan, imminent.

"Baby!" sludged Wizz. He was more American, but also more East London. A confusing combination, if perhaps not for him. "Hi, Suey."

The loft had been organised for him by the firm, he said. A huge open space, with other rooms leading off it. Only five floors up, it was reached by a cranky elevator Susan was afraid would stall, or fall. She was generally afraid of the elevators in New York. Of travelling up and down hundreds of floors, with the legacy of all the cable-snapped crashing elevator cars she had seen in thrillers.

The floor of the expensively furnished loft was of naked polished wood, with rugs strewn over. "See those patterns – Native American Indian." Ranks of windows looked out over buildings which, in day's sunlight, would burn rose-red and cobalt. There was a domed jukebox on one wall, which flickered lime green and played scratchy, ancient numbers for a dime – or was it a quarter? "Art Deco, see. Brilliant," said Wizz.

Anne and Susan got ready in the big, brand-new, black and gold bathroom – there were two bathrooms – where there was a pair of black and gold washbasins, and also a pair of black and gold lavatories. "Anne – does that mean two people go to the loo – at the same *time*?"

"I guess so," glittered Anne, Americanly. If she was offended, nothing showed. (It was only years after Susan learned that two-looed bathrooms were not the U.S. norm.)

The bath in the big bathroom was also big. When full, you could put your head on an air pillow and float about in it.

Wizz drove them to a restaurant. "They call New York Pig's Paradise," said Wizz. "You can get any food here. Anything in the world – French, Italian, Thai, Hawaiian, Sudanese, Jewish, Japanese. And I gotta take you to Chinatown."

The restaurant was overwhelming. It seemed full of black light, with spotlit tables, tall white lilies, impeccable, automatic waiters. Susan propped her eyes open. They seared with tiredness. She felt fluey.

Wizz and Anne drank and drank.

"Don't give her any more wine, please, Wizz. She'll have a hangover."

Susan didn't want any more wine. Or any dinner. She already felt sick from the need to be asleep.

Everyone else in the restaurant was smart and beautiful, wide awake, and sometimes loud with confidence. Susan grew smaller, but not in the correct way. She knew she was too fat, her skin pebbled, her hair not right, her clothes all wrong – how had immigration let her in?

In the morning, she was still exhausted after eight hours sleep. But they had to be up and out by ten, because Wizz wanted to take them 'around'.

The days became a kaleidoscope crush of events, food, places, moving figures, information: of a terrifying elevator ascent of the Empire State Building, the zoo in Central Park, the Brooklyn Bridge strung with pearls of lamps, subway rides. Cops with their guns in their belts. And they seemed always to be eating, too. The coffee shops and restaurants Wizz chose were high-class, with menus like novels. Even the dim burrow under the red banners of a smoking Chinatown, was select.

They stood and gazed up and up, at Wizz's instruction, to the tapering reflecting heights of glass mountains, while below humanity rushed through the canyon, and the yellow taxis zipped like angry bees.

And there were the dress stores, Wizz waiting to pounce with his American Express Card, where the assistants said to Anne, "That is just gorgeous on you," and to Susan, "I guess the bigger size is in order." And the dresses sticking like toffee to her shame-and-heat tacky back, and never quite fitting, regardless.

Height on height, slight on slight, humiliation on humiliation.

She was overweight in the country of physical perfection, and sixteen. And – it went on and on.

"Come on, wake up. You got just half an hour to shower and get ready. Put on the white dress Wizz bought you."

"It doesn't fit. I'm tired."

"No. Come on, Susan. We're driving out to Penn today, have you forgotten?"

What did she afterwards remember of Pennsylvania? The hours-long drive. Fields. A bridge over a river. City night; skyscrapers, and a forgotten movie in an air-conditioned cinema so cold she shivered. They stayed in a hotel. Susan's room was pink. Across the hall, Wizz and Anne made love.

Susan dreamed of driving, or being driven, forward, onward, endlessly.

Back in New York they went to the Cloisters and the Met. Inexorably, Wizz escorted them. The Met had an exhibition, what was it? Great suits of Eastern armour, perfumes wafting on electric breezes. Girls slender as pencils.

"We could drive out to Washington DC, if you like. Take a look at the ol' White House."

The Statue of Liberty swirled in a greenish miasma of fog and jet-lag.

"You can't have jet lag still. We've been here over a week. And I didn't have it at all. Buck up, Susan. You're being a drag."

"I didn't want to come," Susan said, humbly.

"Yes, I know that. And now you're intent on cutting off your nose to spite your face, aren't you."

Then Wizz had to be at work, in something called the Anchor Building on Broadway, the New York branch of the firm. He took Anne with him, wanting to show her off. Susan was also meant to go. That morning her period started, early and painful.

She imagined Anne telling Wizz why Susan couldn't go with them.

Yes, she had told him. He winked at her as they went out. "You poor messed-up women," the wink said, "I can guess what you go through. Lucky me to be a man."

Susan thought how the male Jews thanked God every day for not making them female.

She thought of thanking God for not making her Wizz.

In the afternoon she felt much better. She felt she could breathe, even in Wizz's loft.

Alone, she played the juke-box, leaned from the window and watched the streets below She began to think about America, what she had seen of it, to acknowledge the excitement of it from a distance. If only she could have been here without Wizz being here. If only without the threat of Wizz, and, the future with Wizz, hanging over her – but with whom? With Anne? Alone? Yes, perhaps alone...

Sitting on the four-seater white couch, Susan thought about Anne saying, "How can you stay behind in England, Susan, if I go to live overseas? Tell me that. I don't care if you are sharing with this Jo. You're sixteen and a minor. I'm legally responsible for you."

"I could lie about my age," Susan had said. She did not add, Like I lied all the times you were out at night and I had to pretend you were next door.

Anne had concluded, "Don't be stupid."

The American afternoon went quickly.

Anne had declared she and Wizz would be back by four from the Anchor Building. They were catching a show that night. However, when the elevator clanked to a halt by the doors at four fifteen, only Wizz walked in, in his sharp light suit.

"Where's Anne?"

"Oh, Wilde made a big hit. She and Eve Frenowsky just clicked. Gone off to Maceys. She'll be back in a while, calm down."

Wizz went to the Coca-Cola machine that stood by

the water dispenser, and got two ice-cold cans.

He drank both of these, walking slowly around the main room of the loft.

Susan grew frightened. She could always get frightened of things, but especially now she was frightened of Wizz, of being alone with Wizz. She didn't know why. It was like that other time in England, in the kitchen.

She was scared too in case he took off his jacket and shirt. That had happened already, one morning, seeing him roll from the bathroom in just pyjama bottoms. His body was good, muscular and brown, except at the waist, where it bulged a little... He was also very hairy, his back was hairy. His back scared her most of all.

But now Wizz only walked about. Then suddenly, he turned, and came towards her. He sat down opposite her on the blue couch, which faced the white one.

Susan felt her heart hammering in her dry throat.

She could smell the faint bad smell she always associated with Wizz and knew couldn't be there.

"Look, Sue, let's have a talk, shall we?"

She stared. He was waiting. She managed to say, "Oh, yes, if you like."

"Well, you know, Sue, it's not really what I like. I just think we oughta. Okay?"

Now Susan was the one to wait.

She could see him, studying the floor rug, thinking, mulling it over. Then he looked up, and his pale eyes settled on her face and she couldn't glance away from them.

"There ain't no nice way I can put this, Sue. You've been a right little fucking arse-wipe, ent ya?"

The elevator, which so far had never fallen, now plummeted through Susan's ribcage into her intestines.

Even if she had wanted to speak, it wouldn't have been an alternative.

He wasn't talking loudly. He was quiet and level. So she had missed a bit, too, from the shock.

"… you here and tried to give you a real good time, but you won't have it, will ya? You just can't handle it, can ya? But you see, Sue, your mother means a lot to me. And I want *her* to have a good time even if you fucking poker-arsed bloody won't. So let's make a deal, okay? Let's just say it was your time of the month –" (even in the abysm of terror she writhed with embarrassment) "and now you're gonna be like a normal fucking girl. Okay? Like any other girl with a great mother and a guy like me trying to make it special for her. Not like some fucking little constipated tart. Is that it, eh Sue? You're constipated? That can turn a girl into a bitch. Take something for it. I've had enough of you. You were like a fucking wet weekend from the word go. Little bitch. Jealous maybe. Well, I can see that would happen. You're no oil painting, eh, Sue? With those big spots all over your face and that fat body like a bloody porpoise. Christ, I look at her and I think to myself, Where'd she get this kid? Your dad must've been – he must've been a real prince. But you can't help the way you look, I guess. They might even get you ironed out over here. They can do that, you know. Get girls like you looking halfway human."

All this venom, squeezed out, bit by bit. So level and

controlled. Not raising his voice. This hatred. As if he held her there and vomited, slowly and methodically and over and over and over her.

She thought, in a giddy whirl of horror, *I must get away.* But her legs were leaden. She couldn't move. The ton weight of his vomiting malice held her there in place.

"...see what I want now, Sue, is you act like a proper girl. You act like you appreciate what I done. What *she* done for you. She deserves a life, Sue, don't you think, after mollycoddling you for the past sixteen fucking years. So pull yourself together, girl. I want to see a change in you, I really want that, Sue. No. I expect that. Okay."

Then he stood up. She had thought he would never ever stop. But he moved off, and as he crossed the loft, through its strips of red westering sun, he began to whistle softly. And then he was gone along the corridor to the bedroom he used with Anne.

After a while, Susan too got up, very slowly. She found she could walk. So she walked into the bedroom he had said she could have. She shut the door, and sat on the bed. Then she shut her eyes.

Susan visualised Anne coming home. Trying to get Anne alone. Telling Anne what Wizz had said. Susan knew she would not be able to. It could never happen. She knew she could never speak of it, to anyone.

And he too must know this. That she could and would never speak of it, that she would, from now on, try very hard to appear as he wished her to, and that she must fail. But still, she would try.

He had split her apart from Anne as even the act of

birth had not done, and Susan understood that exactly, even if the thought did not enter her stunned, reeling mind.

Alone? She was. She thought anyway she might be afraid now of Anne, too. Since Anne belonged to Wizz, was a part of Wizz, like that thing in *Hamlet* about husband and wife being one flesh – *therefore my mother*.

By the time Anne got back, triumphant with Macey's bags, Susan was all ready for the show. She had put on the ghastly white dress, which rode up over her fat hips. She had painted out the large round stones of her spots, two more of which had come up since her talk with Wizz.

"All set?" cried Wizz. He was buoyant as a balloon, lightened of his load.

Whenever he was 'nice' to her through the evening, Susan thanked him. She tried to smile and the smile cut her face like a knife.

In the interval of the show she went, (alone) to a cubicle of the ladies room, and retched and retched, embarrassed also by the noises she made, and by the kind woman who, when she came out, pale and sweating, said, "Are you okay, honey? Was it something you ate?"

Which was, in a way, quiet apt, for if not precisely eaten, certainly swallowed.

"I *thought* you were going to be late," said Jo, "and you are."

"Sorry. The train didn't come for ages."

"Well, let's get cracking then, it's just down this road."

English autumn, no longer fall, the yellow leaves hung out from the trees. It was raining, and cars splashed through an overflowing drain on crystal tidal waves.

"I thought your mother must've delayed you."

"Oh, no. No, that's all right."

"She didn't mind, then?"

"Oh no. No. She may not be going, anyway."

"Fallen through has it?"

"Maybe."

"My dad says you can't ever trust a Yank. He learnt that in the War."

"He isn't a – I don't want to talk about him."

The houses were in a terrace, each one narrow, with pointed purplish roofs.

"We're number 17, Flat 3."

Their room was about the size of the main room in Anne's flat overlooking the common. Here the two girls must do their best, with the two mattresses, the gas rings, the light which would flicker like a gas lamp and was always going. With each other's contrary personalities. The bathroom one floor down. And with the wit of the jovial father of Jo, who sometimes called on them to bring them things they 'might need' and catch them out.

"Will your mother want to come over?" Jo asked, that first morning. "Will she want to look round?"

"No, I don't think so."

No, Susan didn't think so. Anne would soon be back in the States, but Jo wasn't going to know that.

Susan had lied to Jo, ably. Long practice. *Oh my mother's only at a neighbour's. She's only in the flat by the common.* But the flat by the common had already been given up. Next month someone else would live there, and Susan would only have to pretend, now and then, to visit.

"If you don't let me, I'll run away."

"Oh Susan don't be so dramatic. And silly."

"I mean it."

"What is the matter with you?"

"I don't want to go. I've said. I want to stay here and go to art school."

"You could have fooled me."

But Susan did fool Anne. Even when Anne said, "Is it still this idiotic thing you've got about Wizz –?"

"I haven't. I got over that. We had a chat one night." Susan, her voice coming cool and steady from far off. "He's all right. He'll take care of you. It was him really. He said, if I wanted, I ought to start making my own life."

"He – said that?"

"Yes. And he said how he felt about you, how he thought so much of you. So I feel I'd just be in the way."

"Susan, that isn't true –"

"Yes. Oh come on, Anne. You've never had a life either, have you? Go on, go with Wizz. It'll be great. Everyone here can think I'm eighteen, except at the college, and they'll think you're still in England. It will be okay."

Anne phoned Wizz long distance.

Susan would not even listen to her voice, speaking to Wizz over the Atlantic wires.

But at length Anne came into her room. "He said let

you."

Susan said, airily, "Told you."

"I said you'd said you liked the talk you'd both had. It made you more confident in yourself. He laughed. He sounded pleased. Well... you've never had a father, have you."

"Oh, look at that sparrow on the sill," said Susan. "Look, isn't it sweet."

"Susan, you *will* be all right?"

I always was, when you left me. And if you don't leave me now, if you make me go and live with him, I will never be all right. I will die.

"I'll be all right, Anne."

Anne's grey eyes, startled, evasive. "If anything doesn't work out – you must write – no, call me collect – reverse the charges. I'll show you what to do. And I'll be over, often, of course I will – we're bound to be. I'll send you some money. The grant isn't much."

She's glad.

I may never see her again. Is that possible? Oh yes. She isn't mine any more. She's his. What I'm seeing now, this woman with grey eyes and dyed red hair, it isn't my mother.

"Oh, don't cry," said Anne. "What am I to think now? *I* don't know. What should I do?"

But she did know, and she would do it. And the tears meant nothing, not grief really, a reflex, like that drain overflowing in the downpour.

III

Patrick was like an animal which changed its coat for the season. In summer he tanned quickly and easily, the long thick hair, that hung most of the way down his back, turned gold, his eyes a light brown. But in winter his eyes darkened like his hair, while his skin paled. Then he resembled, in his long black leather greatcoat, a straggler from some nineteenth century war. He was well-built and slim, but only about three inches taller than Susan was today, in her flat sandals.

She looked at him covertly. It still half surprised her, to see him there, to be with him, even though they had gone around together for over fifteen months, and had sex regularly.

Fierce May sunlight hit the pavement. She was glad they had left the crowded, noisy pub – but was not quite so sure, however, about their intended destination.

"Patrick – you really do still want to go over there?"

"Yes."

"It'll be three buses from here."

"I thought you said the train, then the bus."

"Oh. Okay."

"What's up?" he said. He spoke kindly, but she knew he had made up his mind and would lose patience if she now tried to dissuade him. He would say, justifiably, she was making a fuss about nothing, and look, he'd brought his stuff, and the painting stuff too, and so had she, so what was the problem suddenly.

And what *was* the problem suddenly?

Last night, sitting over their glasses of beer and wine in the Silver Tavern, she had touched, without thinking, on the subject. Finding him interested in what she said, which always inordinately pleased, foolishly almost inebriated her, she had gone on and on.

"This place. Sounds visually fantastic. Especially with all those trees. Could it still be like that?" he had asked.

"Oh, I'd think so. More like it really. More overgrown and so on. They weren't into domestic stuff, just cats."

"Three years ago."

"About three years."

"So, for a *donation*... They'd let me paint there, wouldn't they?"

"What would you donate?" she had asked playfully, glancing into his summer-golden eyes.

"A fiver. Why not? And give them a painting maybe, for their jumble sales. Anyhow, they'll remember you."

"They might not," she said carefully. "I only met that woman once, and I've changed a lot. I was only sixteen."

By then they had walked back to Patrick's room in Belmont Court. Sitting on the floor with the coloured candles lit, they discussed their – Patrick's – plan. By midnight, when they lay down together on the bed, it was all decided. The next day was Thursday and life-drawing, but everyone already knew the regular model had bronchitis and might not come, which would mean improvised still life of something unappetising, like stacked books and chairs. They were into their third year, both worked generally with application; blind eyes were sometimes turned to absences.

After their lovemaking in the bed, with which the room was furnished, and as Patrick slept, Susan lay looking up at the two authentic plaster roses in the high ceiling. The electric wiring was tied off there, only the roses remained, like the ornate acanthuses at the big room's corners, and in the halls outside. Then the last candle flickered out. An odd thought came to Susan as she drifted asleep, that the plasterwork had actually physically vanished now it was no longer visible.

Belmont Court's old Victorian lift woke her, as it always did when she was there, clanking up and down from six thirty a.m. onwards.

Susan got up, used the bathroom on Patrick's floor, and left. It was only twenty minutes through the early streets to her own room – space no longer shared with Jo, or with anyone.

Susan's room though was not so gracious as Patrick's, nor did she have Patrick's small fridge, and the milk, left under cold water, had gone off in the warmth of savage May.

She had arranged to meet him in the college pub at noon. They would have a sandwich and a drink and then set off for the house. For the house that was, which had once been her grandmother's.

Even in the bright morning, gulping back Nescafé

and washing underclothes in the grubby bathroom downstairs, Susan did not feel any qualms about having elaborated to Patrick on the jungles of the vegetable house. Or about travelling over there with him later, and asking the cat women if they could paint in the wild garden, or stay overnight a couple of nights in a sleeping bag, on one of the empty floors.

"After all, it's your rightful ancestral home," had said Patrick, jaunty. "From what you said, they're not going to object, unless we evilly molest their cats."

How had she got on to speaking about the house, the garden, her grandmother? By nine the next morning, she began to wonder, but couldn't recall. Of course, Susan had mentioned Catherine to Patrick before, just as she had told him rather a lot more about her elusive mother, Anne.

Patrick himself seldom commented on what Susan revealed, though he listened thoughtfully. But then he rarely made comments on anyone, apart from their looks. He was always more interested in appearances, objects, views, the things which were integral to his work as an artist. He was, she thought, a very good artist, an active artist. For herself she seemed only able to copy what she saw to a more or less adequate degree, but Patrick – reinvented.

He hoped to get to one of the top schools in London after his time at Silverguilds, to which he had anyway migrated, halfway through Susan's post-foundation first year, from Manchester. But they never discussed that at any length either. Just as they never discussed any protracted or developed union between them, or its cessation. Sometimes, when she caught herself surreptitiously watching him in shock, Susan considered if they, as a pair, were bound to go anywhere beyond their present condition. Really she did not think so, could not imagine it. The future was endless, but indefinite. Even now, she never made demands or suggested extensions, such as their living together. That was from a sort of lazy fear of his possible – probable – unwillingness. And from disbelief too, for Patrick never seemed entirely real. Though she admired him, was quite happy when with him, he also placed a definite sense of duress upon her – because he was another person. He was a stranger. Susan thought she didn't understand him, could never do so, beyond the most obvious elements. Perhaps she did not try. She was, in a way she did not fully know then, and only saw years after, afraid – not only of upsetting or offending him – but *of* him. Of his presence in her life.

So, to lose him simply inevitably through the course of time and events was a miserable idea she did not dwell on, but one which also brought her a feeling of relief.

As she pushed another T–shirt into the canvas bag, Susan realised she didn't want to go to Catherine's house.

Between one thrust into the bag and the next, her mood was altered. It had seemed all right, mildly adventurous, last night or earlier today. But now it seemed – wrong.

She knew it would be difficult to change Patrick's mind. That much she had learned about him. He was absolute in what he wanted to do where it concerned his work.

The first time he had come up to her had been to do with his work. She had already seen him here and there in the college building, next in the pub. Although she was casually friendly enough with members of her class, she had made no personal friends, no one to nudge about Patrick, "Look at *him*," as other girls did. Then Patrick was moved into Susan's class, and at the second coffee break, he came over to her table and stood next to her, only one inch taller since she was wearing her boots with heels. "Can I sit here?" She said he could. Other tables were quite full. She thought it was that. Then he said, "I want to talk to you. I've been looking at you. You've got this wonderful face. You're like a Mediaeval painting – do you know the ones I mean? Only you're prettier. I'm just so drawn to your face. I'd like to paint you. Could we do that?" The combination of politeness and calm effusion was arresting. And exhilarating. All the times after that when they met, had a drink, and then went to Patrick's flat where he sketched her, Susan thought the end of the painting would be the end of their connection. But by the time he had primed the canvas, he had also kissed her, standing barefoot on the earthing utility carpet of his room, holding her in a circle of his arms.

Presently, "I'm sorry, I'd better say now, I'm not on the Pill."

Patrick had been unfazed, indeed munificent and gentle. Susan had been nearly businesslike. Anne had seen to it her daughter knew exactly what she must do, and which, therefore undone, had resulted in Susan.

"I can wait," he said.

Susan visited the Family Planning centre the next day. She took no chances, and observed the full four weeks, while the Pill became effective, before allowing herself to make love with Patrick. Armed with knowledge, Susan was not shy or disillusioned by the pain of her first times, or the seeming unpreparedness of her body. She thought Patrick's body very beautiful, with its lightly muscled spare maleness.

She was also no longer ashamed of herself physically. The shame had gone with an alteration in her shape, both physique and face, that had somehow happened during her foundation year. Though her body was heavier than those of many of the girls she saw, her form had acquired contours, an indented waist and smooth belly, and breasts which, she had suspected, and which Patrick soon showed her, were lovely. The acne had also perished, due perhaps to her total avoidance of cheese, which she had one day read, in a dentist's waiting-room magazine, might trigger spots. Her clear skin was very white, luminous. Better even than Anne's.

Even so, sexually, Susan felt herself awkward, and eventually inadequate. As pleasure began regularly to overwhelm her on Patrick's bed, she noted a curious limitation in herself. She was so completely and utterly satisfied always. Surely there was more to the act of sex than this? What she was looking for she didn't know. Love? Perhaps. But then it would have to be the great hopeless yearning love of obsession or fantasy, which she had felt brush her in earliest youth when only unattainable beings off a screen were the fodder of her desires.

Sex, as she had it, was like eating. You were hungry, you ate, enjoyed the food very much, felt good, went on to do something else.

For Patrick it seemed to be the same.

They were not, perhaps, very experimental – but why did they need to be when fairly straightforward caresses and positions brought such exquisite paroxysms? Nor was it some sort of sexual acrobatics which Susan craved. As with everything to do with Patrick, she did not ultimately evolve a theory, or dwell on any of this very much.

At the station, as on the bus, they bought their own tickets. The train seemed exciting, as if they were going away together on holiday to some new place – instead of back into a disintegrated past.

Susan stared at the railway banks of grass, the purple and lemon weeds and white butterflies.

Patrick sat reading a set book from the college. He was conscientious, in an off-hand way.

Then the light became a blond strobe between rows of poplars, and Patrick burned golden, dark, golden, dark...

Why don't I want to go back? I don't want to have to explain to those women about us painting. Ask them if we can. But why does it matter? And they'll like Patrick. They won't mind.

Do I remember her, Catherine?

The image of an old woman, like a hard grey cobweb, superimposed upon the gold-dark-gold of sunlit Patrick.

Perhaps the house isn't there anymore. Like the flats

when I lived with Anne.

Susan thought of Anne, doing something with Wizz in the U.S.A. What time was it there? About eight a.m. Probably having breakfast then, in a coffee shop, or at the bar in the loft. Coffee and bagels, or donuts or English muffins. Or Eggs Benedict.

The last letter had contained a postcard view of Central Park, some news, (like what they ate for breakfast this spring) and some money. Quite a lot of it, in the form of an International Money Order.

Susan thought of the first money order Anne had sent, and how she had decided to break away at once from Jo, though she had only been sharing the room at Number 17 with her for three months. How Jo's face had disapprovingly fallen. How Jo had said, doggedly, "You won't manage on your own, you know. You make a mess. The washing up will be up to the ceiling and you'll get mice." Whatever happened to Jo? She sent Susan a Christmas card, also doggedly, every year, a conservative card with a slightly religious theme, inside which Jo had always written, *Hope to see you in the New Year, Best Wishes, Josie D. Cartwright.*

The train stopped and shadow came, and it was their station.

In fact, the only way to go that Susan could remember was the old one, along Constance Street, into Dun-Captain-Kirk Street, the park and Tower Road.

She was bracing herself then, in Constance Street, for the place where the flats had been removed. Bracing herself more for not caring now, than for astonishment or affront. And then they were walking by the open lunch-time off-licence and Susan saw the two women she remembered from the cats, coming out of the shop, with a pack of coke in cans and a bulging carrier bag. A man followed them on to the sunny pavement.

Both women seemed the same as before, they hadn't changed. Jackie was still slender and boyish in her sleeveless T–shirt that showed pinkly-tanned, rounded arms and neck. Her eyes were jewel-blue, bright. The grey-haired woman had put her long hair into a ponytail but she looked bad tempered still, frowning over her change and a box of Kit-Kats. The man was about thirty, balding and gangly, with an amused face.

"Excuse me," said Susan. She felt self-consciously and fakingly adult, something that had not happened much for two or three years. "It's Jackie, isn't it?"

"That's me," said Jackie.

"And who are you?" barked the other woman, frowning worse.

"Oh, you won't remember me – I was at the house once, and you let me go round, because my grandmother was the one who owned it before. Susan. I'm Susan Wilde."

"No, I don't remember you," said the woman.

But Jackie said, "Hi, Susan."

"This is Patrick," Susan said, feeling she must, at this point.

They looked at Patrick, and Jackie said, "Hi, Patrick."

Then the amused balding man said, "We ought to get a move on, Jackie. Or we'll miss our train."

"You make it sound like the royal train," said the

bad-tempered woman.

"We're going to Devon," said Jackie. "Have to get into London first."

"Ten bloody hour journey by the look of things," said the other woman. "Bloody murder."

"It isn't ten hours," said the balding man.

"Yes all right, Clive."

Susan said, "Is someone else looking after the cats?"

"Oh, the cats are already down there. That was quite a do, I can tell you, six vanloads of the beasts. But worth it. They love the new place." Jackie delved into the carrier bag, took out a chocolate orange and sniffed it like a connoisseur.

Susan said, "But what about –"

The bad-tempered woman said, "We got a better offer than that house. The Devon deal is a bloody mansion, with seven acres attached. We'd hardly say no."

"Cat Sams in style," said Jackie, putting the orange back in the bag. "The old house here is up for sale. But we'll get most of the proceeds from that too, so we've done really well."

Something meowed stridently and Susan saw the man called Clive carried two huge wire-fronted cat-cages, which seemed to contain two or three cats a-piece. His arms were very long; years of transporting such burdens had no doubt lengthened them.

"These are ours," he said to Susan. "They travel with us."

Patrick spoke for the first time. "So, Susan's gran's house is standing empty?"

"Oh, yes. We were actually all cleared out by last

week. Some couple seem to want it, the agents said. They're prepared to do it up, and it will take some doing, I can tell you, after our lot." Jackie laughed, proud of their legacy.

The bad-tempered woman glared at Susan. "And it's haunted you know. Did you know that?"

Susan stood there.

Jackie said, "Mill, why say that?"

Something had changed, nearly indefinable. It was like the first premonition of nausea, or flu. But – up in the air.

"I'm not superstitious, you know that, Jack. But I also know that house was full of something. And the cats knew it too."

"Mildred," said Jackie.

Bad-tempered Mildred said, "Those windows that always opened by themselves. And the noises. You and Bill didn't mind them, but you two sleep like logs. I don't. And things being moved – hidden –"

Patrick said, "You're saying there was a ghost?"

"There was and is psychic activity. We've left, but that has not."

Jackie looked at Susan. "There may have been some odd things sometimes. But none of it that couldn't have a normal explanation. Mildred isn't saying it was old Mrs Wilde."

"She didn't die in the house," Susan heard herself blurt. "They found her on a park bench. She had hypothermia, probably. She was covered in frost. Her heart failed."

Mildred's intolerant face softened as if a blow had spread it.

Susan wished Patrick would say something, but he didn't, merely stood there, looking at all their faces, Mildred's in particular, almost certainly because he thought hers the most drawable face, with all those cracks and fissures of inclement temper sculpted into it.

But Mildred looked at Susan and said, "I'm sorry. I shouldn't have said anything."

"It's nearly quarter to two," said Clive, who still appeared amused, but now with a type of smiley embarrassment.

"Come on," said Jackie.

"Good luck," Susan said.

"Thanks. You too." They turned, moved off, a single entity, garlanded by raucous meows.

"Where are you going?" Patrick asked Susan.

"I want a drink."

"Right. Sure. Then we can get on."

"No we can't. The house will be shut up. We won't be able to see anything now, or get in or stay."

"There's always some way in. We can get over the wall or something. I'm not giving up now."

He stood in the shop and waited while Susan paid for her diet coke. Then he selected a chocolate bar for himself and bought it.

Susan felt a stab of irritation. Why did they always have to pay for everything separately – okay, meals or alcohol perhaps, but a coke – a Marathon – bus fares?

"I don't want to go there now, Patrick."

"Because of what they said?"

"No. I'm not sure."

"She had a marvellously crazy face, that older

woman. I suppose she was marvellously crazy. Anyway, it'd only be your gran."

"She had to be called Grandmother, and her name was Catherine Greyglass. It isn't that. I don't want to go scrambling over walls and getting tetanus and arrested."

Astounded, Patrick stared at her. Then they stood there on the street under the high afternoon sun. Neither of them made a move either forwards or back.

He ate the Marathon.

"Look," said Patrick, "why don't we just go and see? If it's ropey or they've got security, obviously we'll leave it. But the way you spoke about it – I've got a feeling it's just what I've needed for some outdoor studies – and no one else will have anything near it. It really would help me, Susan."

So, they went on.

Of course.

She had gone up to look at the books in the book-room. Despite having been sold once, they were all still there, all those sombre black or maroon volumes stretching up and up, like bricks in the cases. And the long table was there, and on the table the glass dish. In the moonlight, the glass wasn't yellowish but grey.

Something was knocking somewhere, or tapping. Tap-tap. A tree branch on a window in a wind that didn't blow. Or something in the turned-off water pipes.

Hearing it, Susan was not disturbed. Not afraid. Even when the book-room window slid up with a sharp hiss, not even then.

But she had to get back downstairs, and return to the sunken room where Anne and Anne's mother, Catherine, were confronting each other.

Susan didn't hurry. She was grown up now. She went out and along and down the stairs, and when she reached the room, she stood in the doorway, glancing about.

Why had Anne brought her at night? They never came here then. That time before the funeral, even, when they had been each day, clearing up, they had always left the house before it got really dark.

The trees outside were huge, monolithic, and heavily-furred as black bears. Through the crystal panes they cast their ink-black shadows.

There was no one in the room, no one and nothing. No furniture – not even any cats now, not a single plant.

Then something screamed in a terrifying way. Susan leapt out of her skin of sleep and crashed against Patrick in the depths of the double sleeping-bag.

"Hey – what? What is it?"

"Oh God –"

"*What?*" He rolled aside and switched on the torch, blinding her with a broad eye of light.

"Something –" she said. "There was a noise."

"It's those cats in the garden. Ssh. It's all right."

She lay down against him. "Patrick, I dreamed about her – only she wasn't in the dream. Only – I think she was. Patrick?" Patrick was silently asleep once more.

Susan looked up where the eye of the torch still flamed on the ceiling of the bare upper room.

Cat's-eye.

Outside she could hear them now, the eerie wailing of the small tribe of cats, which still remained rampant in the eldritch garden. She and then Patrick had counted nine or ten of them in the undergrowth outside.

The smell of cats' urine was still strong in the house, too, but Patrick dismissed it, did not seem to care. He did not mind the several boarded-up ground floor windows, or the leak which had occurred in the drains to one side, and added another foul odour.

They had got in without trouble. Others had already been before them at the gate, breaking boards, squeezing through. The *For Sale* sign had *Under Offer* pasted over. There were no notices about dogs or vigilance.

He had stood on the drive, among the vast architecture of trees and thickets, and the deep green sea of nettles, gazing at dim faded wedges of cut pumpkin walls.

"The colours are like you said – but even better than you described them. It's almost prehistoric-looking out here. The whole thing is worthy of Cézanne. Or – Klimt."

To have pleased him so much should have been enough, but now it was not. She had hoped the outer wall would be impassable, and then, when it wasn't, that he would hate the house, be repelled.

The garden, where, during the afternoon and evening, they had come to see the cats, was what involved Patrick most, the glimpses of the house slotted into boughs of cabbage green foliage.

He left Susan quickly and suddenly. Taking his sketchpad and a handful of crayons and pencils, he was off, dumping his rucksack beside her in the grass, so she felt she had to stay to guard it.

Then she saw him too in glimpses, climbing a terrace by a pool clotted with enormous fretted angelica leaves, between the bay trees and the holly and rhododendrons. He sketched, leaning at angles, matching the angles of the house, perhaps.

Finally Susan dragged the bags to one of the side doors. Standing outside this door, she could not recall it. With all the boarded windows, only the colours of the house – as Patrick had partly said – were really as she had recollected them. Ivy was growing in festoons along brickwork and drainpipes.

She thought the door would be locked. But it gave. Very likely the others had already broken in.

Patrick was by then up an apple tree, among the last of April blossom.

She shoved the bags inside the door, then sat down on the path in the sunlight, her back to a wall.

Later, she began to see the cats, some black and white, and a tabby one, then three gingers, moving singly, or poised in groups behind ferns or high grass. They must be escapees from the flight to Devon. Had Jackie known?

Somehow – I don't remember that apple tree. Did they plant one – a mature one? Oh, he's climbing down now. Nor that monkey-puzzle up there. They always look man-made, monkey-puzzles, but by someone very artistic. Made out of papier mâché, then covered with prickly black velvet.

The sun shifted. The path sank violet with shade and it became colder.

At last Patrick walked over. "Don't you want to make any drawings?"

"No. Thanks."

"Okay, let's take the bags in. See where we can sleep tonight."

"Do you still want to?"

"Sure. That's fine." As if to please her, since *she* wanted to, which she had (feebly?) tried to tell him she did not.

"This light," he said, "is so good. Look at the sunshafts. I'd like to set up for a quick study with paint – just gouache. Before the light goes."

It was after five-thirty. Beyond the doorway, the house gaped in cracks of shadow, split with long passages and the side of a staircase. It looked totally unfamiliar. Susan might never have been here before. Changed so many times by the on-building of Catherine and Richard Wilde, did the house still go on altering itself, adding parts, shifting rooms around?

"I'm hungry," Susan said.

"Yes, I am. Did you bring anything?"

"No. You do the bags. I'll go down to the high street. What do you want?"

They decided on fish and chips, and he said keep the bill, he would give her his share when she came back.

"It's all right," she said briskly. "Anne sent some money. I'll get it."

When she and Anne had lived in Constance Street,

they took a different route to reach the high street. She almost thought of doing that now, to make the walk longer. But that would mean going back through the park, and they had crossed the park earlier and it had subtly depressed her again, it's barren openness, its increasing irrelevance.

Westering sun lay brazenly along the roads. The roar of homeward traffic rushed like the sea.

Homeward, she thought. All those people going home.

Susan thought of Anne, of going home to Anne in the various flats. Of nights when Anne stayed in and taught her card games, or they read books, curled in the armchairs, or watching TV, and sometimes ate toasted cheese sandwiches with grilled tomatoes before going to bed. Susan never ate cheese now. A small price to pay for good skin. But even so, one more fun delight forever lost.

Had she been happy then, as a child, with Anne? Yes, quite happy.

As she stood in line in Chiporama, Susan weakly regarded her nostalgia for a past only some three or four years away.

Wizz had stopped the past. Sliced it clean through. As she had known she wouldn't, she hadn't seen Anne since. Oh, seen photographs Anne sent, there had been a ton of those, usually with Wizz – on a beach in Florida, at a wine-tasting in New England... that sort of thing. And she and Anne had spoken now and then on the phone, but seldom, for Susan's phone was always a shared one in a hall, and unless a time was scrupulously pre-arranged – and stuck to by Anne –

the phone was not often free.

She looked happy, Anne. Always slim and vivid, well-dressed, tanned, her hair still undergoing metamorphoses – *Do you like this short style? Wizz says he likes it for the summer.* And, *Don't you think this curly mane is neat? Eve fixed it for me. We had a ball.*

Wizz too was tanned and well-dressed, and looked a bit fatter. But Susan tried not to see him in the photographs. Because of Wizz she pushed them all into a box at the bottom of the curtained-off rail that was her wardrobe. Because of Wizz, and not wanting to see him, even the ones of Anne on her own. (Husband and wife: one flesh.)

When Susan got back to the house with the fish and chips, a bottle of wine and a cheap corkscrew, Patrick had vanished deep into the garden.

She thought of eating her fish first, before locating him. The food was almost cold by now anyway.

But then she went to look for him.

The garden never struck her as anything but abnormal. There was something more than verdancy or undiscipline about it. Prehistoric was Patrick's word, but an apt one.

Briars clawed at her, rose bushes that had become tall hedges, all thorns. Paths tunnelled through the black green cavities between terrace-sides, clumps of giant docks, and trees whose roots had cracked up the paving as if a bomb had fallen.

"Here I am. You wandered right past me."

"I've been trying to find you for an hour."

She thrust the fish and chips at him. She didn't know where they were, in some insane wilderness or forest, staring out through a sort of hole in the trees, at a ruin with boarded-up windows, while the sun died and the sky turned khaki.

"You seem fed up," he said.

"I am."

Did he even hear her? Yes, he heard, and was sympathetic – but indifferent. They were two separate people. They were bound to have unlike states of being. It didn't concern him. Painting did.

His painting of tonight was slapdash, watery, effective. They drank the wine.

The sky looked better now, a blue-grape dusk with some stars. Now and then, as the shadows meshed the garden into solid darkness, the whitish forms of two or three cats glimmed and faded.

"What a wonderful place," he said.

"Is it?"

"Don't you think so? We were lucky, getting in before they started pruning and cutting down and wrecking everything."

But the wine made her feel better. The wine said, Oh, it's all right.

"That house," he said, "is strange, isn't it. I just put the bags upstairs. There's a room there with some old curtains on the windows. People have got in. Someone had a fire in a fireplace, recent, could have burnt the house down. How many rooms are there, do you know?"

"No, not really. I told you, my grandparents built a lot on."

"Why didn't you get the house, Susan?"

She glanced at him. In the dusk, Patrick too was a

shadow, with gleaming cat's eyes.

"I said. Anne and Catherine didn't get on."

"I wish you had," he had said. "I wish it was yours."

"So you could come here and paint it," she said.

"Yeah."

And the wine said, Oh, it doesn't matter.

Perhaps the wine, or the greasy fried fish, caused her to dream of the book-room. And of the sunken room below.

For a long while after she woke from it, Susan lay tensely, with the torch-splash above her like a parasol of useless hope, listening to Jackie's cats courting and fighting in Catherine's garden.

Then she must have slept again, because she woke up and bright light was coming in at the threadbare curtains.

Had she dreamt anything this time? No.

Patrick, though, had.

"I was following this old woman all through the house," he said to Susan.

"What old woman?"

"Well, I thought it was probably your grandmother."

"You don't know what she looked like. What did she look like in the dream?"

"Well," he said, "really more like that one we met in the street – Mildred."

"She wasn't like that."

They ate the now-stale buttered rolls Susan had also carted back from Chiporama, and drank some coke he had brought. Susan offered him the money for her coke, and he accepted it, even though she had paid for the previous night's meal.

None of the taps worked in the upstairs bathrooms, but downstairs, he said, was an old cloakroom, where the cold tap was still on for some reason.

Susan did not use this cloakroom. She had squatted outside in the rhododendrons to pee, and would attempt nothing else until they went to the nearest pub at lunchtime.

During the morning, Patrick worked again outside, somewhere in the garden, and Susan sat again on the path by the house wall, in the sun, reading a novel. She was bored and uncomfortable, unwashed and indigestive. She kept thinking about Anne, and her own childhood. Not Catherine though. She did not think about Catherine.

Then there was a noise behind her, above her, up in the house. It sounded like someone easing up a window. Susan stayed where she was. Then she rose and walked out, and down as far as the apple tree, and stared back and up through the towering evergreens, to the upper storeys. But nothing seemed to have happened.

They took their bags to the pub; they had both said it would be unwise to leave them behind. Besides, Susan needed her sponge-bag.

Patrick put down his beer glass. "Do you want another?"

"Yes, please. No, not wine – here's the money. Could you get me a gin and tonic?"

When he came back, he said, "I think there's someone in the house, Susan. Apart from us, I mean.

You know I saw there'd been a fire lit. I could hear someone walking about this morning, before you woke up. Very soft. And then when I was painting, I saw someone at one of the windows."

Susan drank her gin. "Who?"

"Couldn't see. Just someone looking out."

She thought of Anne, and the other flat, with the balcony and the ashes of the day and the first time the name *Wizz* had been spoken. What was *Wizz* meant to mean? A whiz-kid. A *Wizard*?

Patrick said, "I think I'll call it a day. And you don't want to paint anyway, do you. And maybe it's not that safe hanging about there."

"I thought you loved it," she said, "and didn't care."

"Why are you narrowing your eyes like that?"

"Am I?"

"I've just done enough," he said, dismissive. "It's all the same, isn't it? All the views are alike. Let's go back. We could go into college. Or just stay at my place." Surprising herself, she felt rebellious. She wanted to say, No, now *I* want to go to the house. I want to make love in the garden, and rush indoors and scare the squatters and light a fire and dance on the bare floorboards.

"All right," she said.

He's boring me, she thought, as they sat in the train. Is he? Not how he looks, he looks amazing. And his painting is great. But – this not talking about anything. Not doing anything.

He isn't interested in me. I'm not, in him. I want to be, would be. But he never lets me see. I don't know –

Even so, they gravitated back to Belmont Court, and

had a bath, and then had vibrant sex. That evening there was a party, and they went to it, Patrick incredibly handsome in his white shirt with the straps. And she thought, This is all right. It doesn't matter. Yes.

IIII

Next summer, about two months after Patrick had gone, Anne called Susan at five to midnight.

The moment she heard the phone rattling down in the house, Susan knew it was Anne. Perhaps because it was one of Anne's times – her times of return in the past.

"I'm sorry, did I wake you?"

"No. I think you woke a couple of people though."

"Too bad – or are they giving you grief? Tell them it's your mother."

"It's all right, really. How are you?"

"Wonderful. I'm wonderful. Or Wizz says so. It's evening, about seven here, and ninety in the shade. We're going to dinner with the Sepplevines – I only have a moment. But I just wanted to let you know. I'm coming over next Monday."

"Over… "

"To London. What do you think?"

"That's – are you? Is Wizz coming too?"

"No, can't. We're having the apartment done up, he has to be around to monitor the builders, and anyhow he's up to his eyes at work. But he said I should have a break, come and see you. It's just a trip, about five days, I think. But we can meet and do things. English things. I bought you the most sensational dress this afternoon. I won't say what it cost. Wizz said you ought to have some New York clothes."

Susan's voice, which had sounded only mildly affable and concerned when she spoke of Wizz, now sounded mildly enthused. "I can't wait to see. But Anne – you do know I'm generally a size sixteen."

"Oh, these are fine, baby, don't fuss," said Anne. She had never lost her English accent – which was apparently very popular with and intriguing to all their U.S. friends, even to taxi-drivers and waiters in bars. Only her syntax had sometimes altered. "Look, honey, I'll call you Sunday night – a bit earlier – when I confirm my flight. Okay?"

"Yes. I can't believe –" Susan heard herself saying, her voice now suddenly puzzled and unsure, "that I'll see you. You really are coming?"

"Still Susan," said Anne. "Why else am I phoning you up at the dead of night?" She seemed tickled, herself excited, in all her whirl of active and opulent life, that she was going to meet her daughter.

They met in London, at Anne's small, plush hotel by Regents Park. Susan was nervous. She had put on a loose black summer dress which made her look slim, and showed off her white skin that never browned, try as she sometimes had, and pale gold sandals, and earrings, to be festive.

Anne came straight down to the foyer. Once Wizz had looked like a film star. Now Anne did.

Her hair was very short and sleek and ice-blonde, shining and expensive. The cream linen dress was expensive too, entirely plain. On her left hand, but not on the wedding finger, was a square-cut and brilliantly faceted emerald, as big as a five pence piece. Her golden hands had pearl-white nails.

She was immensely, and seemingly totally, tanned. She looked as if she had been dipped in liquid amber, and brought out evenly coated. But as they drew closer, Susan noticed the sun had also cracked Anne's surface here and there. They were couth, fine cracks, but they were cracks.

"Honey!"

Heads had turned already anyway. How Anne looked, walked, her clothes and ring, her costly scent. Though the hotel was a place for the moneyed, not many of them, for all their dollars, had managed to look like Anne.

Susan hugged Anne carefully, afraid to spoil her immaculate veneer. Anne had no such reservations it seemed. Her embrace was warm and strong – hard. Her body felt hard. Susan wondered why, for Anne had never carried any superfluous flesh.

"How are you? My God, you do look sweet. Look at you. Your face is so pretty, Susan. And your lovely eyes. Why didn't you ever send me a photograph like I asked you?"

"There were never any really nice ones. I kept waiting for a really nice one –" (Actually, waiting for Anne to stop asking. How could Susan send a photo of herself that Wizz might, even for a split second, look at?)

"But now here you are. Susan Wilde."

Anne's eyes were alight. Not moist, but vivacious and full of excitement.

She's more excited than I am.

"You're not feeling tired?"

"Oh I never have this jet-lag stuff. I sleep on the plane. I feel fantastic. Let's get some lunch, I *am* starving."

Anne drank a vodka tonic (no longer gin) and Susan a glass of cold white wine, as they leafed through the pink and fawn menus. It was nearly two o'clock, the restaurant half empty, but no one hurried them of course.

"I can't believe you. My God, Susan. Look at you. It's been almost four years. Why wouldn't you ever come over and see us?"

"I wanted – it's just – the college, and the holidays are so short to get anything arranged. And they give you holiday projects to do –"

"Yes, yes. Well you're nearly through with that. Come in the fall, yes? We'll lay on the red carpet treatment."

"Mmm. Thank you. Only I may have to do an extra course then. One of the tutors, Rod Ayres, he wants me to do a specialist course on design, book jackets, that sort of thing. He knows some people in publishing." She added the mysterious proviso, the Masonic code everyone seemed to grasp but herself. "It could mean real work, a job."

But, "Rod Ayres?" said Anne. "What an English name."

"I think he's Irish."

"Well, but what happened to your Patrick?"

"Rod's a *tutor*. I still see Patrick," Susan lied.

"He sounded very fuckable," said Anne, jolting Susan. "Now I've embarrassed you. I get used to the States. Our crowd is pretty open in what we say."

"We – yes, we have sex together."

"And you're on the Pill. Good. Thank God for intelligence."

They ordered. Susan grapefruit and then grilled chicken, Anne smoked salmon and steak with mashed potato.

"So what is Patrick going to do after college?"

"He's already got into the Royal College of Art. He's actually there this year. They raved about him, so he started early."

"Impressive."

But Anne had lost interest in Patrick's prowess as an artist. Would she have been more inclined to hear details of his sexual abilities?

Susan thought, I don't know what to say to her. All this is so stilted.

Perhaps extra alcohol might have helped – but after her vodka Anne only drank water with the meal, so Susan did that too.

In any case, Anne then took over the conversation, effortlessly at last. She spoke about America, and about Wizz, about cities and landscapes, about going to Canada last fall, (the spectacular leaves) about their friends, and their friends' houses and apartments, that all seemed to be in areas named things like this or that Heights.

The last time Susan had been in London was with Patrick, after the Royal College had accepted him. They had gone out (splitting the bill) for a meal at a steak-house, and afterwards he hadn't invited her back to his new flat, they had just walked along the Embankment, and parted at Charing Cross, presumably for ever.

"Let's go shopping this afternoon," said Anne. "But first come up to my room. I want to give you all the things I've brought you."

Up in the room, drink became available again, a bottle of Smirnoff, ice, glasses, tonic and limes. A waiter conveyed this, and on his way out Anne tipped him two pounds.

"Try this on." Anne didn't work now. Like everything else, including the lunch, Wizz had in fact bought all this, everything.

The dress was red, with a halter neck, low in the back and very short. The vaunted price must be in the silk, not in the *amount* of silk.

Susan got into it, feeling uneasy, not taking off her bra, which then looked tacky and ridiculous. But the dress did anyway. It was too red, too showy. However, it did fit.

"It's great, Anne. I'll wear it to the next party."

"Wait till you see the blue one. Yes, now your eyes are blue. But I like it when they look grey. Mine have got greener. But yours are like mine used to be."

There was also a make-up kit, a miraculous object, like a child's paintbox, which seemed to have all the colours in the world, even turquoise mauve for the eyes.

Anne drank another couple of vodkas as Susan struggled to get through her single. Then Anne stopped drinking.

"I have to go down to Brighton tomorrow. Something Wizz asked me to drop off to a business colleage. Wizz wants me to meet this man, his wife –

charm them, Wizz said. They have a big house, Tudor, I think Wizz said. I'd ask you to come, but they might think it was a bit much, two of us turning up."

"That's okay. I should go into college tomorrow."

"All right. But I'm only here six days. When I get back Wednesday, come up and stay. I'll book you into the hotel, yes?"

"Yes, yes great."

"It's so strange," Anne said, "seeing you. You know I'm hardly a possessive mother. But you're not mine now. You're your own person."

"Am I?"

"I'm impressed with you, Susan," Anne said. "The way you stuck to your guns. I mean, about staying here. Getting on, on your own."

A desolate wave rolled in through Susan, and retreated, leaving unidentifiable sticky flotsam behind on her inner skin.

"This house I have to get to is at some place called Rothsdean. No, it isn't Tudor. I can't remember what Wizz said it was."

Abruptly Anne's perfectly managed face changed. It seemed to loosen, and sag a little on the firm bones.

"I'll tell you. I wasn't going to. We had a bit of a fight, Wizz and I. One of the reasons he sent me over, to make up for what happened. I probably shouldn't tell you."

Susan didn't know what she was expected to say, or feel. Did the idea of Anne and Wizz falling out aggravate or please her? Not please. It wouldn't have – it hadn't – lasted. Was anyway – too late.

"We're over it all now. That was in June. He had a

little fling, shall I euphemise. You're *slow*, Susan. I mean he was screwing someone else."

"– oh."

"Yes. Oh yes. I found out because the damn girl wouldn't let it go. Kept calling him up at the loft. I said to him, Who is this bimbette called – would you believe it – Madison, who keeps calling you? He said, She's from the office. She's dumb, forgets stuff all the time, calls me to ask me. Then one afternoon I came back with Eve, and there was this Madison, standing downstairs, and she said to me, I have to see Wizz. And Eve went scarlet. And, well, I figured it out finally. The little dope made a scene, then I told her what I thought of her. Then Eve took her outside and shooed her away. I don't know what Eve said, but it was effective. And when he came back that evening I tackled him."

Susan sat gazing at Anne. Had she ever heard Anne so voluble?

Anne said, "He admitted it. Straight off. He said he was sick of her, couldn't get rid of her, had been trying. It just happened one time he was away alone and she was a stand in for his regular assistant, Chloe. I guess Madison made all the running. Do you know, this Madison was the ugliest little bitch I've ever seen. She had bushy black coarse hair, all over the place, and little girl shoes. Skinny. I mean so thin you could snap her in half. And glasses, let's not forget those. She is blind without them, I gather. But she was kind of young, you know," said Anne heavily. "Only about twenty-five. I couldn't miss that. I said to him, If you want younger women, let's call it quits, Wizz. And – he started to cry. Well, we made it up. It's okay now. Really, it's okay now. And we went to Bermuda for a while. And then he said, let's get the apartment done, fresh start, and he said, You go and see that girl of yours. Tell her to come over. And he bought me this ring. Did you notice the ring?"

"It's beautiful."

"It's vulgar," said Anne. "Or it would be, if it weren't an emerald. He was talking about diamonds, but I said I am not Liz Taylor, Wizz. You note, the finger. I never wanted to marry. That wasn't the deal."

By the time they left the hotel it was late to shop. They wormed in and out of boutiques tucked in among white pillars, then ended up after all in the park, watching ducks and having cups of tea at a plastic table.

"I miss this," said Anne. "That exact wet green in the water. Just that shade. It isn't ever like that, there. I don't know why. I'm crazy. It's just me. Wizz says England is like a back garden, and the States is the real world."

This is my mother, Susan thought.

Really, this is Anne.

Then the ducks did something quaint and spontaneously they both laughed and for a second it was the past, on-going uninterrupted time that had never shifted, and then they stopped laughing, and it was gone again now, and different, not the old Susan and Anne, but the new Susan and Anne, with Wizz and the Atlantic still between them.

When Anne didn't ring on Wednesday, Susan thought she was undoubtedly at last tired, after the journey to and from Brighton performing Wizz's errand, on top of the flight. Thursday came and began to go. Susan phoned the hotel. "Ms Wilde? Yes, she's due back Saturday."

Saturday was the set day for Anne's departure.

Susan thought there must be some mistake, and resumed waiting for Anne to ring her. Was she worried? She told herself she wasn't. But even so the little gnawing knot in her stomach that kept her from college, and haunting the downstairs hall for the phone, did not make her feel anything for Anne – but a little gnawing knot.

On Friday morning Anne called.

"Susan, I am so sorry. No, I'm still at Rothsdean. It's been an experience. Oh, I wish I'd brought you with me, Keith said it would have been fine – I should have risked it. This house, it's like a stately home. Genuine Georgian. The Prince Regent, it seems, used to visit. In acres of parkland. There's a boating lake. I've had the most fantastic time. But, God, Susan, I'm sorry, I'm not coming up to London again, there just isn't time. The hotel is sending my stuff down, Keith arranged it all. A powerful guy, I may say, and she is very nice. Susan, it's just too much hassle, you see, and I can get to Gatwick so easily from here – they've seen about changing the flight and everything – look, I have to go. I will write you as soon as I get back. And you'll come over and see us, Wizz and me, in the fall, won't you? That's a must."

Rod Ayres tired Susan, talking always about the 'technical side' of drawing, reducing art relentlessly to a kind of mathematics. He was thin and smelled too much of aftershave. Though over fifty, she thought, he had begun to seem interested in her in an amorous way. At first she hoped it was just his manner, then she realised from things said to her by other students, that they were considered to have something 'going'.

Susan became increasingly frustrated, feeling she must keep in with Rod Ayres to ensure fulfilment of the Masonic code of the Job, but wanting to avoid him. He knew she was no longer unavailably involved with Patrick.

As Rod lit his fifteenth cigarette, his voice droning, Susan thought of Anne, re-installed by now in Manhattan with the straying Wizz. She thought of Anne's odd new garrulousness, her rhythm of talking which seemed to have altered so much, perhaps only inevitably mirroring the phonetics of the people she now spent all her time with. The mirror too, obviously, of Wizz.

"So, we'll go and see old Mike, see what he can suggest. Then maybe I'll take you for lunch, eh, Susan."

"Oh, I can't," she said. "Sorry."

Rod looked displeased. Affronted even, as if she had loudly burped or spat at him.

What was she supposed to do? If she simply said, I'd hate to have lunch with you, or anything else, he would cease to assist her up the ladder of Work.

"I have to see a relative."

"I thought your mother was now in the States

again?"

"Yes. I have to visit my grandmother," Susan said.

"Your grandmother? Do you have such a being?"

"Oh yes."

Why did I say that? Never mind. His ruffled plumes were settling.

"Keep the old folk happy, eh," agreed Rod, refusing to see that to Susan, and the other students, he was one of the happy-needy old folk, too.

So, I'm coming to see you Catherine.

Sitting on the train, alone this time, Susan did not feel strange. She felt slightly amused.

Another day off college, but then, she'd have lost far more of them if Anne had returned and she had stayed with her at the hotel.

But what, really, was she doing?

After the bus and train, another bus, then Constance Street, which now meant absolutely nothing, and then the other street and the park, which was full of a schools' match of football, boys shrieking and jerseys. And Tower Road. But Tower Road was meaningless, too. The vast houses looked smaller and a lot of trees seemed to have been scythed down. Even the two great oaks on the grass as you approached the final wall, had been viciously pruned, and had produced hardly any summer leaves.

The witch's house. The vegetable house. The Labyrinth.

Susan loitered along the wall. It was stripped of most of its creepers, the stonework tidied up. The *For Sale – Under Offer* board was gone, and the old iron gate was gone, replaced by a new green-painted wooden door, with a name in iron letters on it: *Borders*.

Why had Susan come here? Why had she come here the other two times? Patrick had wanted it last time, yes, but it was more than that. She could have resisted. And she had come here before then, the first occasion, when Jackie and the cats had Catherine's house.

Was it the lure of the past, where things were safer since they had already happened?

Surely, the past hadn't been in itself that appealing, *not* safe, or really ideal in any form.

Did this always happen? Any previous time, however dull or bad, was going to seem better than the time you were stuck in now?

Susan opened the green door by its natty metal ring, thinking as she did so of the green door which led to the Afterlife or astral plane in H.G. Wells.

And the door did open. Not surprisingly, of course. Deliveries, postmen, Jehovah's Witnesses would need to get in.

The drive had been cleared substantially, the trees cut close, as if pushed back. Things had a glossy, well-kept garden look, and framed by their widened avenue, the house broke clear, shocking Susan. It too had been stripped and cleaned, and repainted a bold, dazzling primrose. There were shutters on some of the upper windows, polished blue, like the front door.

A vague rumble she had been aware of now solidified into a moving machine, some sort of small excavating digger, trundling out around the far side of the house. Earth sprayed about it. She could see anyway, as Patrick had predicted, dense vistas of growth had vanished. Open space was in Catherine's garden now, spatially marked by the poles of so-far surviving trees.

I'm trespassing.

What now? What now?

What did she want from this ever-metamorphosing place?

As she walked along the drive between the neatly manicured plants, the gaps of ground from which nettles and docks and briars had been wrenched, Susan formulated her plan. A silly plan, and why anyway do it? But why do anything – it was all a sort of game, with intractable yet deadly-inane rules.

There was a bell, as there had been in the days of Catherine and Mrs Danvers. It shrilled through the house in a horrible attempt at two melodic notes.

At the same moment the digger started to make enormous gulping sounds.

No one would hear.

Standing there, Susan realised the stained glass panels of Catherine's door had been incorporated in this other one. She thought of wading through the pool of coloured lights inside, jade and crimson, the last okay part of Sunday before her grandmother.

The door opened.

"Ye-es?"

Susan felt herself blushing, but took no notice of it, carried on. (What point was there ever in taking too much notice of the constant betrayals of the body?)

"I'm sorry to bother you. I'm looking for Jackie – she used to live here, the cats charity, Cat Samaritans –"

"Jackie. Oh yes," said the woman who had opened

the door, her face in turn betraying her, too, hardening and seeming fixed and intent. "Yes, I've got her address somewhere, Devon, I think. Come in a minute. I'll have a look."

"So you knew Jackie?"

"Yes – I had a cat from her."

"Of course. Yes. We had to contact her about some of the cats that were left behind. They kept on sneaking in and fouling, which was a bit of a drag – the house was nearly a ruin, you know, not kept up at all – and we were trying so desperately to get everything fixed, and the decor sorted out."

The decor in the wide hall was now Pale Milk, (Olivia said) with one Coffee wall and some Chinese Red accents. In the side room where they now were, a large room Susan didn't recall – perhaps made out of two rooms knocked through – it was darker Coffee, with notes of Royal Blue, and kaftan upholstery.

Everything smelled immensely clean, slightly of paint still, and of induced aromas, *pot-pourri* and scented candles, and the vast cloud of roses and freesias in a black pot by the fireplace, (which had green marble inlay.)

Olivia rummaged vigorously through some old address books from a bureau. She seemed one of those effortlessly groomed, youngish women that Susan had always marvelled at on TV, or in London – they appeared to spring out of bed or the shower sparkling, and fully clothed, the make-up minimal on unblemished matt skins, and their hair washed and made delicious in the night by pixies.

Olivia's hair was long and densely blonde, as blonde as Anne's had been, but this looked natural. Unlike dyed hair, the roots were of a deeper, gleaming platinum colour, by the hairline and the casual, perfectly-designed robot parting.

Susan watched Olivia with envy and some uneasy visual pleasure. Olivia was the Unattainable State, the patently *other* kind, as were her conditions, her persona, everything about her.

She had told Susan quite a lot, quite quickly and fluently, as if telling strangers who she was came quite naturally. Her husband, Jeremy, was in the City now in his twelfth floor office above the Thames. A girl – an au pair, Susan deduced – that Olivia seemed to call Dosha, was due to come in and bring them coffee for which Olivia had shouted lightly along the hall.

"Here we are. Yes. Now – Jackie – I can't read the second name, Jem's awful handwriting – but I expect you know... look, see if you can make it out."

Susan took the book and carefully copied out Jackie and the cats' address in Devon, on a piece of paper from her bag.

While she was doing this, the girl who must be Dosha rushed into the room.

"Dosha – gently, gently –" said Olivia. But her voice oddly had an edge of something that did not, suddenly, belong to the flawless Olivia-Jeremy World.

"Olivia – it's there again – it's there on the stairs. I see it when I am coming to go out of the kitchen – and then the faucet spouts on in sink –"

"Dosha," said Olivia, "calm down, please."

But Dosha only poised, a dark-haired slender girl of

about Susan's age, waving her hands and her eyes wide.

"Oh dear," said Olivia. She glanced at Susan. "It doesn't do anything, Dosha. You know that."

"It is *there*."

"Yes, it's there. Look, go back and get the coffee. It'll be gone by now. It always goes as soon as we see it, doesn't it."

"I don't want to see it."

"No, but you have and now it'll be gone."

Dosha slunk out of the door.

Olivia turned round and looked at Susan. Her own eyes were big and frank. "We have a ghost, you see."

Susan said, "Do you? Really?" She sounded polite, quite interested, pragmatic but open-minded.

"Actually, Susan, I was hoping – as you knew Jackie a bit – that you might know something about this – oh this *bloody* house." Olivia flushed angrily. She stood up and flexed her well-shaped legs in their tailored jeans. "When I think of the K's we've poured into it, the mess it was in. And the garden, they're still working on that, and the landscape gardener – all these things we've had done. And then no sooner did we get in the bloody place than all this starts. I thought it was a poltergeist, but Jeremy says they're always caused by young children – and we don't have any kids."

Susan felt now as if she were not necessarily operating her own body. As if she were only sitting up inside her head, like Jeremy in his office gazing down like God on the city and the river.

"What happens?"

"Oh – just lots of unimportant *awful* things. All the

time. I hoped it would stop. I had a friend in, she works with crystals and that sort of stuff, professionally. She exorcised the house for us, she got the energies going the right way – or so she said. But it actually made things worse. Look, did Jackie ever mention –?"

"Well, yes. She said there was a knocking sound and windows opened by themselves. And Mildred – one of the others – said that things went missing –"

"They *do*, Christ knows they do. I lost my first wedding ring – I mean the ring from my marriage before I married Jem. I don't wear it, I keep it in a box – and then it was gone. And I thought for a minute Dosha had – well it was terrible, because she's a darling girl, from Helsinki, and she would *never* – and when I got that sorted out, the ring reappeared – *under* the box, where I'd looked – but then my jogging shoes went missing – *jogging shoes*. And oh, lots of things. And yes, there are sounds. Not knocking, I haven't heard that, perhaps Dosha has – more - sort of *breathing – pacing –*"

Susan stared. She saw that Olivia was pale, Pale Milk, like the hall without the splash of stained glass window light thrown there.

"But the worst thing is, we do see things."

Susan no longer felt removed. She felt as if she were trapped, one of the lesser stars, in a horror film.

"What?" she fumbled out.

Dosha came in wobbling a tray of priceless coffeepot and cups, and some exotic biscuits. She seemed calmer now, as Olivia had told her to be. Putting her tray on a coffee table, Dosha said, suddenly, "It has gone."

"It always does," said Olivia. But she had by now frightened herself out of any pretence at organisational cool, and Dosha stood there, shaking her head bleakly.

"Mr Jeremy say," said Dosha, "he has never been the one of us to see this thing."

"No, he hasn't, the bastard. He never sees it. Or hears it. He says it's possible, but won't believe *we* have it. He thinks I'm mad. Dosha's mad. That we're hysterical and affect each other and imagine it. Even about the ring, he said *I'd* lost it."

"What is it," said Susan, "that you see?" She didn't want to know.

Dosha spun round and stared at Susan wildly. "Up on the stair, out in passage. Or in rooms. Once in my room – is on the wall – like a *fly*–"

"Yes, she saw it in her room, didn't you, Dosha. And I have, in the bedrooms and even in Jem's study. Down here, everywhere."

Susan heard herself again: "Is it – a person?"

"No," said Olivia surprisingly, and with abrupt flatness, most of the energy seeming to leave her. "I can't describe it. It's – a sort of absence of anything else. Like – oh, if you look at something too bright and there's a dark patch on your vision a few moments. Only not like that. And then taps turn on, and sometimes lights, or they go out when they're on. They fuse all the time, too. At least Jeremy has to believe in *that*."

The coffee sat on the table. They all looked at the coffee, not making a move to try anything with it.

Susan said, "What will you do?"

"I hoped you might know something. I haven't had

the courage to ring up Jackie. Honestly, I'm afraid of what she might say, after the thing with the cats."

Susan said, "I do know an old woman used to live here, once." As she said it, she felt the hair rising on her own scalp.

The digger outside had fallen quiet again. An enormous silence filled the house, a stillness as if time had come to a stop.

"An old woman. Oh God. And I suppose she died here."

"No I don't think she did."

"Only that was it about the cats. Let me explain. Even though this will sound crazy. Crazier. Cats were in the garden, a lot of them, about fourteen. I saw them, Jeremy saw them. The *builders* saw them – some of them left bits of food, which Jeremy put a stop to. But the cats got in anyway and peed up the walls, apart from screaming the place down every night. So I called Jackie and said could she do anything about the cats she'd left here, and Jackie said they hadn't left any cats, they were all accounted for. So I said it must be a feral colony then, that had moved in when the house was standing empty for a few weeks, what a strange *coincidence*, sounding sarcastic because I didn't believe her. Then Jackie said, of course a few cats had died during the years they were here. Old ones or sick ones that didn't make it. Which got me thinking, because by then I'd heard the noises, and Dosha had seen something in her room – Oh, I don't know. I just know I'm bloody sick of it."

Dosha had by now sat down in a chair done in complex jazzy russet weave.

Olivia said, with fresh sharpness, "Coffee, Dosha."

Then Dosha got up, and poured out coffees and handed them round with the biscuits.

"Could you get a priest?" Susan said, lamely.

"*Tried* that. They won't come. We're not Catholic, anyway. They're the only ones who pay attention to ghosts or demons. And what have we got? An old lady and some cats."

Susan said, "She really didn't die here, the old lady. She – I think she left the house and went into the park and they – she was found on a bench. It was cold."

"Christ."

Dosha said, "That's why she is here, then."

"Oh Dosha," said Olivia.

"She has to come back she thinks, though she should go elsewhere, for she's dead. So she goes the wrong way, and is stuck now."

"No, Dosha. Just shut up."

Dosha said in a low stubborn howl, "I have written to my uncle. I am to be going home."

"All right, Dosha. Let's talk about it later with Jem."

Out in the wide hall, the light had moved from the glass in the door.

Susan looked around. The entry into the other succession of rooms had surely been moved, it was further along. On the blank of new wall thus provided, hung a sepia photograph of a Roman aqueduct.

But she thought of how she dreamed once, of Catherine, in the sepia photograph she, Susan, had perhaps seen, or not.

"She was called Catherine," Susan said. She felt ashamed.

Olivia looked at her, evidently wanting her to go now, and to forget all this nastiness until the next thing happened.

"I mean the old woman. Catherine."

With no warning Olivia turned and shrieked violently, malevolently into the ringing body of the silent painted house: "Go to hell, Catherine! Clear out, Catherine! Fuck off! Fuck the fuck off!" Then turning back to Susan, no longer quite flawless, and hair ruffled, her eyes like those of a scared bacchante, Olivia murmured, "Great to meet you, Susan. Take care."

Book Two

V

This isn't for me. It's for Flat 6C."

"I know. She's out again. Can you take it?"

Susan looked at the postman's pale, stare-eyed, harassed face. "All right."

He, or one of the many postmen who came and went, was always pushing letters for Flat 6C through her own door, which was marked, obviously confusingly, 6E. This however was a package, not very large, but too big to fit in either door.

6C was directly across the hall. Susan had never glimpsed the occupant, although she knew her name from all the wrongly-delivered-letters – Ms Crissie Fielding.

Crissie Fielding, the only truly adjacent neighbour, was very quiet. Which was also explainable if she was out a lot. The faint strains of popular music or TV that frequently strayed from the other flats, (6A, B and D) down the corridor, never emanated from 6C.

Susan took the package back into the kitchen.

Sitting at the small table, with her half-eaten croissant, she glanced over the package. Apart from the address, it bore a small label. G.D. Register.

Vaguely, Susan felt reluctant to confront

Crissie-of-the-unusual-spelling Fielding with the package. (Before it had only been a matter of putting post through the letterbox.) Why on earth?

Perhaps meeting anyone, here, talking to anyone, here – which generally, so far, for a whole seven weeks, Susan had meticulously avoided – was going to feel peculiar.

She had after all met so many people here, and none of them the original person, which person she had met over and over until she was nearly thirteen, but never met, *never,* in any real sense of the word.

Susan was thirty when two quite major things happened in her life. First she won the Cameron Award for Book Cover Art and Design, a prize that made her dear to Paragon Books, and also enhanced her bank balance with an astonishing ten thousand pounds. The following month, at a party thrown by Paragon, she was introduced to R.J. He was the writer whose work had had her prize-winning jacket.

"I liked your cover," he said, rather stiffly, "thank you."

After all the fulsome praise, this sounded grudging and awkward. Susan assumed R.J. had not liked her cover for his book at all.

It had been a difficult novel to exemplify. Ornamental yet subtle and convoluted, but having to have Paragon's required bold, eye-catching image. In the end Susan had constructed the artwork from layers of cut and pasted paper, a method she hadn't employed for some years. The three main characters of the book, represented in this glowing, yet ghostly and fragmented way, seemed to catch the eye of everyone, the prize committee included.

Susan was never sure what she thought, but then she never was with her own handiwork. Sometimes, looking, months or years after, at covers she and other people had only thought adequate, she sensed genuine effectiveness. Conversely, jackets which had been enthused over repeatedly, seemed lacking in anything save the careful draughtsmanship she had learned.

She still thought of herself as a fraud who had somehow managed to fool them all, Paragon in particular, that she was a bona fide artist. In the beginning, when she had had to work full-time in Paragon's art department, and was herself commissioned only to execute one or two covers a year, Susan had thought this was probably her proper station. When more cover work came her way she was always sure she would soon be found out. And since the award, she lived in a sort of ironic guilty alarm, waiting for the clock at midnight.

"I'm sorry, I did try to reflect something of the novel, but I felt I hadn't. It's a complex book. And mostly in – quartertones. The watercolours I did though, were hopeless."

R.J. gazed at Susan over his glass of red wine. He still looked preoccupied, but seeming to hear her now, if from a great way off.

"But you won the Cameron," he said.

"Yes. That was wonderful."

She felt self-conscious at confessing to him what he must already know, her failure to do justice to his work.

She also felt frightened of him, had done so as soon as she saw him, a thing that hadn't happened for approximately a decade.

R.J. was forty-four, as his book jacket copy told anyone who cared to read it. He was tall, about six foot three, and heavily built, though it was bone and muscle, not excess flesh. He had an olive complexion, like a Spaniard or Greek, neither of which he was, dry dark curling hair beginning to lose its pigment, and bloodshot golden-yellow eyes like a bird of prey.

"Your glass is empty," he said next.

"Yes. I don't want any more wine."

"Let me get you an orange juice," he said, and turning round plucked one, she thought, fantastically, from thin air. This he handed to her. "No," he said, "I did like your cover. I didn't recognise it, that's all."

"No."

"But you get used to that, and at least it was attractive. It was elegant, in fact. It reminded me – not of art but music. Bach, totally precise yet cunningly split in overlapping sections."

"Your book reminded me of Chopin, the piano concertos," she returned boldly, because she felt timid and refused to be. And because he had said something that might have been pretentious, but it was not, and she wanted to aid and abet this, somehow.

"Really? Chopin. Why?"

"I can't explain. It's sadness… the under-orchestration – I don't understand music technically."

"And you *read* my book too," he said. "Few illustrators bother to do that now. They just want a note of what to draw. And my God, you've helped sell it for me, you know."

Then he half turned and said, "Oh, that's my wife signalling. I'll catch you later, Susan."

Rod Ayres had actually got her the job at Paragon. Or, his 'friend' Mike Hammond had done so. Mike had leafed through her folder as Rod perched on a chair-arm, a fifty-year-old avuncular teenager. "There's some pretty good stuff here, Susan. And your qualifications are fine. Now, you've done this design course, you say?"

Susan, on Rod's suggestion, had done six months by then of the course, for which the council had refused her a grant, but Anne had sent her money.

Rod said, "She's a star pupil, Mike," and Mike had looked at him, and long after, when Susan was working for Paragon as a dogsbody in the art department, Mike had said, "Do you still see Rod?"

"Oh, no," Susan had said.

"That's probably as well. I think he was a bit serious about you."

And embarrassed by it all, and by Rod, she had said forcefully, "It wasn't ever anything like that. He was my college tutor, that's all." But Mike only shrugged.

Of course, there had been the inevitable scene, after she got the job, when Rod insisted – that was *insisted* – on taking her for a meal in an Italian restaurant.

He ordered a bottle of wine, (the first of three) at once, and before the food came downed three large glasses. He kept talking about the divorce he had had from his wife 'last August', stressing he was a free man, saying the things he would like now to do, such as going to France or Rome to paint in the summer, trying to entice her.

They ordered desert, which Susan didn't want, but, "Oh you must. Go on. Look, they've got Death-By-Chocolate –" disappointed when she only selected a fruit salad, and saying, "God, I hope you're not trying to lose weight, Susan. You're lush and lissom, you know, just right –" so she felt herself redden. Rod had the chocolate death, spooning it up like a famished child. Then he reached across and took her hand.

"You'll come with me to France, won't you, Susan?"

"To France?" She looked blank, surprised. "Why?"

"Why. You know why. I thought you understood what I've been trying to say."

"No," she said dimly.

Rod still didn't give up. He leaned towards her in a wave of Mandate and said, "I really like you," in an eager young voice.

"Oh – I'm sorry. I didn't realise."

"Don't be sorry. Now you do."

"You see, I'm – *with* someone."

He looked at her. Then he drew back. "Oh yes?"

"Yes. We've been together for a year."

"You never mentioned it."

"Well... I didn't see how it was relevant."

"Come on."

Ashamed now of herself, (though why? It wasn't because she was lying) she looked away and said, "I'm sorry. But Joe and I are living together."

"Joe."

"I'm in love with him," she rushed out angrily. "I'm not going to want anyone else."

Rod looked both squashed and belligerent. "I think you might have said. I've been trying to help you."

Susan wanted to say, So you wouldn't have helped me if you thought there was nothing in it for you? But she said, "Yes, I know. Thank you. You've been very kind." And then, fawningly, hollowly, "I'd never think someone like you would be interested in me."

"Why not?" he roared, making other people turn and stare, to add to the jollity of the occasion. "I'm too old, is that it?"

Then he pushed back his chair, which drunkenly fell over, threw some notes on the table, and walked right out of the restaurant. Leaving her to settle the bill, which after three bottles of wine and the deathly chocolate was considerable; the twenty pounds he had flung down did not remotely cover it. Luckily Susan had meant to go to Sainsbury's on the way home and brought extra cash.

About ten days after this, a letter arrived. *'Dearest Susan, can you forgive my irrational behaviour?'* It hadn't been, she thought, at all irrational, perfectly logical. *'I know the situation with your boyfriend, but I'd still like to see you. Nothing heavy. Do say you will– '*

She tore the letter up and put it in the bin.

Two weeks later, receiving a now regular monthly pay cheque, she had moved into another flat, where she would not have to share a bathroom. She did not send Rod Ayres her new address.

Following the Paragon party, where she had met R.J.,

Susan began work on a cover commission for a difficult manuscript she had been trying to read without much success. Something strange occurred. The book's anti-hero had dark curling hair and eyes described as hazel. Though in his late thirties, the anti-hero now assumed the lineaments of R.J. And suddenly, Susan could read the book. She tore up her provisional sketches and started inadvertently to draw R.J. She had been warned before never to use the appearance of any well-known actor, even where the author likened a protagonist to one. Houses had apparently been sued.

Susan did draw R.J. however, several times, on a sketchpad. The drawings dissatisfied her, naturally.

Four or five nights after the party, she dreamed she and R.J. were walking in London; somewhere, she thought, near to the British Museum.

The next morning he called her.

"Hello, Susan."

She knew who it was and her breathing stopped. She said, without a breath, and uncertainly, "Hello…?"

"I'd like to talk to you. Is that possible?"

"…yes."

"That's good. Shall we meet for a drink somewhere? Do you have a place you like?"

When she went to meet him that evening, the compendium of terror and joy she felt worried Susan almost in proportion to her exhilaration.

She kept saying to herself that undoubtedly he only meant to discuss something to do with business. Perhaps he had a contract with another publishing house and wanted her for another cover, there, which might cause bad feeling since she still worked part-time in Paragon's art department.

Now and then too she reminded herself he was married, and had made no secret of it in front of her.

He was waiting for her outside the wine-bar, greeted her with a grave, absorbed face, and opened the glass door for her to go through.

They sat in a window, looking out over the river and its lights. It was spring, the dark still came early.

"That was nice, that you agreed to meet me. I like your dress very much."

"Thank you."

"But then, I like everything about you, Susan. Look, I'm not going to muck around. I'll just say it straight, and then if you're not interested, we'll finish our drinks and part friends. Okay?"

Stunned, mesmerised, Susan nodded.

"I'm married. I think you saw my wife. She's a lovely and intelligent woman. I won't say I've never had any relationships outside our marriage before. But it's only happened twice in twenty years. Frankly, they didn't mean that much, and both were some time ago. Then, I met you. I'd like to know you, Susan. And I'd like to make love with you more than I can say. I felt there was something between us – or was I just being presumptuous?"

"No."

"Good. Oh good, thank God." The smile broke through his face, relieved and flame-like, dazzling her. "But is the fact of my marriage a problem for you? I know it should be. It should be for me, and in a way it is, but – well. I realise this isn't a very salubrious offer."

"I don't care," Susan said.

She didn't, not then.

The wine-bar was lit by an intense bright lambency, which increased and increased, because she could plainly see it shone also for him, he felt it too.

And when he took her hand, her blood filled with a tingling sexuality that travelled through her whole body in an instant, waking every inch of her skin, outside and in, undeniable and irresistible, making age, marriage, even life, irrelevant.

It was one of those part-time days when she still put in at Paragon. When Susan got home, in the black December evening, there was the package for Crissie Fielding sitting where she had left it, on the table in the kitchen.

Susan looked at it. Then she poured herself a glass of white wine from the fridge. Taking the glass and the package through into the main room, she sat down there.

The main room of this flat was large and very beautiful from its proportions, its faultless ivory walls, and the high, high, ceiling, which was painted a translucent lavender. None of the floor-length windows were square, but Gothically arched at their tops. In here, one of these had an opaque, smooth white pane, set about with round jewels of purple and topaz stained glass. This window would have looked out on the entry and a wall, a dark space the architect obviously thought was better obscured. But Susan didn't mind the white window; she found its nacre opacity mysterious. The other windows in the room were on the opposite side, French ones stretching from floor almost to ceiling. These gave onto the gardens, her semi-private area. Three steps led down to where, against the evergreen mass of two flourishing firs, a small ivied stone Pan stood on goat legs, playing a syrinx. Beyond the curve of the trees, a green lawn, regularly mown, tumbled to a lily pond and stands of birch, after which bay trees filled the view. The gardens were magnificent, as the agent had proclaimed when showing her round. And though communal to all the flats, Susan had seldom met anyone in them, except the old man with the little dog from Flat 14G. Maybe moving in halfway through October accounted for this. On the other side of the trio of steps down to the garden, was an ironwork bench, coloured deep peacock blue. Sometimes, on an unseasonably sunny morning, Susan had sat there with her coffee. The master bedroom, which opened straight off the main room, also had French windows to the garden, these not needing steps.

Susan tapped her fingers on the package for 6C.

She had come to terms with this flat. In fact, she hadn't had to. Not really. Everything was so changed. And after the succession of rooms and poky 'self-containeds' she had had before, this was a palace. Too enjoyable not to enjoy.

So. The next step was simply to deliver a small light box to a neighbour. To ring her bell, and say, "This came for you."

It was nothing.

Nothing.

Susan put down her wine, got up and carried the package to her front door.

When she opened it, looking across the waxed wood floor of the well-maintained outer hall, she studied the exterior of 6C. Indeed, it was identical to her own door, and painted indigo, like all the doors in this section of Tower Gardens.

("There are, in all, thirty-five flats, of one, two, three or four bedrooms," the agent had announced, grandly. "They seldom come on the market.")

6C was silent, as ever. Was Ms Crissie Fielding even in? Perhaps she wasn't.

Susan took a step across the hall, and a sudden coldness enveloped her, despite the radiator which warmed the corridor.

6C was part of the sunken rooms. Yes, it was. Just as her own flat was, but you would never know, everything had been altered, partitioned, opened out, even the landscape of the garden.

Then she was at the door and she had rung the bell.

And again she thought, Perhaps she's not in.

The first time, they went to a hotel he had found, quite pleasant. They had lunch, which she couldn't eat, and then went up to a comfortable, clean room. The story was they had a plane to catch that evening, and needed to sleep, any luggage having gone on ahead. They acted up to this pretence, but whether anyone believed it, or cared, who knew.

Susan was frightened and nervous when she was alone in the room with R.J. But the moment he touched her, began to kiss her and hold her, and explore her with his hands, the most violent desire flooded her body. She had never felt anything exactly like this. It was like diving into a fiery sea. Her need gave her, too, a confidence she had never known during sex. She lost her politeness, diffidence. Any outer awareness. She wanted him to do all and everything to her, and to do the same to him, and when their untrammelled actions reached their heights, she felt herself let go of everything.

After Patrick, she had had a few brief affairs – they could not be called relationships. She had always liked sex very much, found it easy and rewarding – but beyond the obvious pleasure, unimportant.

It was not that, with R.J., her ultimate pleasure heightened – although she suspected orgasm had changed its aspect – but the act became earth-shatteringly significant. Afterwards she could not stop thinking about what had happened twice in the hotel bed. Just as, from the first, she had not been able to stop thinking about R.J.

They met a couple of times every month, usually Thursdays, sometimes Friday. He lived in Hampshire, and travelling into London could only be managed like this. She wondered how he did manage even this. Presumably his wife, (who Susan knew from the party was called Maria) thought his trips were to do with his writing – jaunts to research, buy books, or visit necessary sites, publishers and agents. Or *did* she think that? Although never asking him, Susan sensed that perhaps R.J.'s Maria knew where he went, even with whom.

Some people had such arrangements. Didn't mind it. Did Maria also have somebody else?

The trouble was, R.J. was nothing to do with Maria,

or anyone else. He was only to do with Susan.

She knew this was absurd. Incredibly they had their separate lives and did not only come into sentience in each other's proximity.

Sometimes R.J. could manage a night, even two, away. Then he came to stay with Susan in the latest of her self-contained Lilliputs, the one in Brashspeare Road.

These were holiday times, sometimes even extending through part of a weekend. They would cook meals in the tiny kitchen, eat out at pubs by the river, walk along the towpaths and over the local common. Their lovemaking grew slower and more sensual. They slept back to back. They told each other things about their lives, things about work and inspiration, and self-doubt, and necessary arrogance, their childhoods, people they had known. No one too recent, though. No one who had been a serious lover. Or a wife.

Sunday, if there had been Friday and Saturday, was always the day for parting from R.J., the day he went – home.

She began to dislike Sundays. There was something unwanted that must be done on them, and the next day was... school.

Susan did think about Maria, of course, inevitably, now and then. She didn't dislike Maria, was not even envious of her. She felt sorry for Maria, in case she was being deceived, and could be made horribly distressed by finding out. And, naturally, she feared Maria, for Maria could perhaps, at a stroke, end the flimsy yet imperishable bond which tied R.J. and Susan together.

Otherwise Susan did not believe their communion would end. It was only a matter of sticking to the rules. Of keeping it quiet, and keeping quiet about certain things to each other, and hoping, without ever voicing it to each other, but hoping for *what*? Maybe Maria would fall in love with someone else. Or she would die, (she was older than R.J. but not by very much.) Then again Susan steered well clear of the banal viciousness of wishing death to Maria. Besides, R.J. seemed, in his way, to love Maria. On the rare occasions when he mentioned her, (then never intimately) it was gently, fondly, and with respect. And, obviously, accustomedness.

The year passed.

Nothing altered.

They met in London – went to one of the two or three hotels which seemed welcoming, and where falsehoods were no longer offered or expected. Or R.J. came to Brashspeare Road and the kitchen, bathroom and 'studio' room woke up and grew bright.

One evening, near Christmas – a solitary strange time always for Susan, led up to by insane parties, socialising, drinking, unreal sentiment, ending in her own Christmas days alone – Susan was making R.J. a private pre-Christmas Christmas Dinner. The turkey was a chicken, but free-range, with stuffing, sprouts, roast potatoes – all tasty things she had learned to cook in the past eleven years, astonished at how easy it was to prepare food simply and well, if not inventively. There were even crackers, in shiny red jackets, and a bottle of Champagne in the fridge.

R.J. said, "I love this, with you."

Susan said, "Do you?"

"You make it fun," he said. "New. But you're young."

"I'll be thirty-one next year."

"As I said, young."

There in the candlelight, and the smoking scents of cookery, he looked, with his hawk's eyes, older, so she abruptly saw. His hair had more grey now than dark. His body seemed unchanged, tawny and muscular still from playing football and running in his youth. Yet, didn't he stoop now, a little?

A shadow of sorrow moved across Susan, as if the bright-lit light had dulled, or the candles, half of them, gone out. He was older than she was. He was the one who might die. One day, not now, but there, there ahead of them.

Susan said, "I wish we could be together. I mean I wish we could live together. Is it ever going to be possible?"

He shook his head. "No."

They had never had such an exchange before. And yet each of them slipped into it as if practiced – could it be he was?

Susan said, "I mean – wouldn't you rather be with me? I mean, would you rather? Or does Maria always come first?"

"No one comes first."

"Which means *I* don't."

"You can't, Susan. I'm sorry."

"Does she know about us?" said Susan, drinking the red wine they had already opened to give each other presents by. And by which they now gave each other this.

"Yes," he said. He was looking away from her. At the small tree she had dressed only last night, for tonight.

"She *knows*?"

"Yes."

"Does she know who I am?"

"Yes. She said you looked pretty and smart. She likes your book jackets."

"Oh for Christ's sake –" Susan's voice had become high and loud, not pretty or smart, or artistic at all.

"You asked me," he said, flatly.

"Yes, all right. I asked you. Why does she put up with it?"

"She loves me," he said.

"And *I* love you, so *I* put up with it. That's very convenient, isn't it, for you."

He got up and walked round the small enclosure of the room restlessly.

She heard the chicken spitting in the oven. She ought to go and baste the bloody thing. Let it wait. Let it blacken.

"Susan, I've never made this a secret, to either of you."

"Very noble."

She thought, I sound like Anne.

She thought, was this how Anne went on to Wizz that time, over that girl – God what was her stupid name – Madison? Anne wouldn't have behaved like Maria. She'd have got hold of me and shaken me to bits...

"I explained. You knew the situation."

"That makes it all right."

"No. But I didn't lie. You could have told me to fuck off."

They stood in silence, R.J. looking at the tree, Susan looking away into the kitchen, hearing the chicken spitting and spitting like a deranged feral cat.

The bell sounded tinny, as if its battery was going.

Susan stood there, holding the package for Crissie Fielding.

Now the hall seemed too hot, though beyond the main front door, only about ten feet away, the December wind was rising, howling in the empty garden trees.

She was not at home.

Susan considered leaving the package by the door of 6C, because otherwise this might become a nuisance, trotting back and forth and never finding the woman in.

The door opened.

Her hallway, similar in size to Susan's, was illuminated by one soft rosy lamp on a side table. Its floor had stayed bare; the same waxed wood as in the outer hall. This, and the pale walls, totally unadorned, bloomed in the rose glow, floating, somehow unusual.

The girl too was limned by the light. It made her a veil around her fair, long hair. But her face, as she leaned closer, caught the low outer light in the main hall. She was beautiful, and like many beautiful things, even people, seemed familiar.

"Hello," she said. She smiled. Her smile was one of familiarity, as if they had already met several times, always happily.

"Hi. I'm from 6E. The postman brought this, this morning."

"How kind of you. Thanks." She was Susan's height. Her slim young hands slid out and took the package. She turned it over. She said lightly, "A gift from an admirer, I fear."

She must have lots of those. She was very slender, wound like a delicious pen in a silvery-white wrap. No rings, no jewellery. No make-up even on that white and unmarked skin. She seemed, from the sophisticated way she was, at least twenty-two or – three. The flat was hers, too. Susan knew very well, no one not well-off or in a lucrative job, could handle these mortgages.

It was an old-fashioned turn of phrase, and an odd thing to say: *An admirer, I fear.*

Susan moved, about to go.

"We've never met before," said the girl. "I'm Crissie."

"Yes, I know from the parcel. I'm Susan Wilde."

"Yes, *I* know too." How did she know? Oh, no doubt more wrong deliveries – which she must have refused to accept for Susan, since she, Crissie, was so often away. "It was kind of you to bring it across. Would you like to come in and have a coffee?"

An appetising coffee smell had come stealing out of Crissie Fielding's flat, along with another scent, equally appealing, fresh but faintly floral.

"I'd like to, but I have to take a call in a minute, from the States. My mother. Thanks anyway."

"Okay. Hope to see you," said Crissie.

Her smile was so carelessly inviting, it made Susan smile back.

She thought, Maybe she is a lesbian, and I'm giving her the wrong impression.

Then Crissie, stepping aside, shook the parcel and said, "I bet this is my Gerry. He will overdo the generosity."

Susan didn't know if she was expected to comment. Then Crissie said, "So long," and the door of 6C glided shut.

She was extremely familiar looking. *Who is she like?*

Someone in the movies, conceivably. But then, not really anyone *now*. More like Vivien Leigh, or the most youthful Jean Simmons – someone like that. A bit.

As she closed her own front door, Susan heard something fall brutally in her kitchen. Going to see, she found a plate had slipped from the rack into the stainless-steel sink. It was in three pieces.

The wind hit the arched windows.

Once there had come the first lesion, others followed. Soon it became a habit with them to row. To begin with he was reluctant, trying to stay calm, non-committal, decent even. He tried to make it up to her, in all the wrong ways – through sex, excursions, even buying her a new TV and video she didn't want. Vulgar and useless things.

They tried too, to be as they were. But that was now too difficult.

Susan became petulant. She whined and could not stop herself. R.J. grew taciturn. Then he stopped meeting her.

Their meetings had always depended on his phoning. He simply did not.

She thought of getting his and Maria's ex-directory number from someone at Paragon, for whom he was again writing a novel.

But what would she do with it? For all her ghastly whining, she did not have the crassness to call up their home in Hampshire. This was partly her fear of Maria and partly her pity, her sympathy, for Maria.

Susan felt sick, from the moment she woke to the moment she managed to fall asleep each night about three or four a.m. She couldn't really eat, lost half a stone in a month, which weight loss by now had no attributes of anything.

Only when she worked on a cover did she lose track of the rift with R.J. – but then only momentarily. And her work was not very good. Like a disobedient child, she was sent back by the editor to re-work the canvas massively, made a hash of it, and had to start again.

"Is something wrong, Susan?"

"No – I'm just a bit upset. My – grandmother's not well."

"Oh, lord. I'm sorry. Yes, you look worn out. Is she dangerously ill?"

"Oh no, no, she'll be all right. She's very strong. But – well. She's the only family I've got in England."

Why such a ridiculous *lying* lie? Never mind, it got her off the hook, though someone else took over the cover job. Too many more of those and Paragon wouldn't want her. Her fame from the Cameron was fading fast. As had the ten thousand pounds.

One night he called her. She thought it was Anne,

who promised in a letter to call at ten o'clock. But Anne seldom now kept any promises to Susan, including the ones of sending her more money orders, coming to England again, or of making it financially possible for Susan to visit New Jersey, where Anne and Wizz now lived. The last, of course, was a relief.

Instead of the by now slightly Americanised, at last slightly aging, voice of her mother, Susan heard R.J.

"Are you free to talk a moment?"

"Yes," she said, and fell back into the chair.

"I've missed you."

She started to cry.

Standing above herself she thought, Shut up, for Christ's sake, just as she had when they rowed and she sniped and whinged.

He said gently, "Don't cry, Susan. Let's – look, I have to come up to meet Hammond next Tuesday. Shall we have dinner? Maybe we could. I'd like to see you.

They met on Tuesday. She wore a new black dress, and earrings he said were like stars. He was supposed to get back to Hampshire, but in the end he rang Maria from a callbox. Susan stood there and heard him say he had missed the train and would stay over at a hotel.

She wondered, even as they travelled to Brashspeare Road, if later he would tell Maria the truth.

This time their lovemaking was hesitant, and in the end, for Susan, disappointing. There was no longer an electric current between them. It was only sex. Had she stopped loving him, being obsessed by him? Or was she only afraid to be?

She didn't care. She had to see him, have him, even

if only now and then, if only for the most methodical sex.

He looked older. But so did she, she thought.

That night, lying in bed with him while he slept, she wished Maria would die, couldn't hold the wish away, like a cruel and unavoidable sneeze. The next day it haunted her.

Sorry, Maria, she thought, after he was gone, at eight a.m. But she cried again.

She cried off and on all through the next months. So that by the night they stopped seeing each other once more, this time for good, she was practice perfect in the abysm of tears.

Susan had made a second bedroom, which opened independently from the corridor of her flat, into her workroom. It too had a large window which looked out over the lawns, to a winter-bare apple tree and the edge of the pond. Some days after she had delivered the package, from this window Susan saw the girl walking across the grass.

Viewed in cold morning sunlight, she was arresting. The long skeins of fair hair incandescent in the sun, her slender equilibrium, and the choice look of her pale clothes. Later, Susan left her flat to go to the supermarket, and saw a white cat running along the corridor towards Flats A, B and D.

She had never seen this cat before, but now and then a few cats appeared in the gardens, pets of other residents, or even visitors from over the walls.

The cat reminded her oddly of Crissie Fielding. She didn't know why. Perhaps it belonged to her?

Susan had asked the estate agent about cats the first time, when he brought her to see the flat last spring.

"A feral colony in the gardens? Not any more. I've never heard of it, I must say. Probably some cat place caught and re-homed them."

He had vouchsafed nothing about Olivia and Jeremy, either, let alone about Catherine. But he was very keen on the virtues of the flat, showing it off to Susan like an impresario with shares.

"Oh. There's no window in the bathroom."

"No, 'fraid not, but there *is* the latest in extractor fans. And look at *this* – " he pressed a switch, and a false window lit up, with a stained glass picture of Rousseau-esque leaves and flowers, reflecting in the midnight blue suite, with its gold sea-shell taps.

When he showed her round the gardens, which were now like a well-stocked park, with pools, roses, terraces, trimmed hedges and trees, statues and vistas, Susan had been perplexed by the exterior of the house. Naturally it had undergone endless internal rearrangements and additions, and had gained about seven main entrances to give access to all the flats, plus all the arched windows, French doors, and balconies. But certain parts of the masonry had also been, she thought, cut into and excised, other portions extended outwards. But she had never been sure of its contours. Even the house had not, constantly changing its shape. Now it had been made also strong and youthful, with a succulent, painted skin. "Mediterranean Gold," described the agent. "But they repaint, when they do the other major maintenance, every five years."

With all the cover charges for the upkeep of garden

and house, the general price, and the vagaries of her semi-self-employed status, getting her mortgage had been quite an endurance test.

Soon after Susan returned from the shop and was unpacking her groceries, her doorbell sounded.

She knew before she opened it – knew also the next scene would contain the white cat.

Sure enough, Crissie Fielding stood there, holding the cat in her arms. Both of them were so relaxed. Not a care in the world or a hair out of place.

"Is he yours?" said Crissie.

"No, no he's not."

The cat purred, and looked at Susan from half-closed bluish eyes. She reached out and stroked his forehead with one finger, but quickly.

"He's gorgeous," said Crissie. "Is he a stray? He looks too sleek. I'd have him, but I'm out half the time. It wouldn't be fair.

"He belongs to 6A or B, I think, hazarded Susan. "I saw him going that way earlier."

"Oh, what a con-artist. And I gave him a piece of ham."

Crissie leaned fluidly down, with a dancer's grace, and set the white cat on the wooden floor.

Instantly he shot past Susan into her flat.

"Oh," said Crissie, "I'm sorry."

"It isn't your fault."

The cat flew along the flat corridor, and bolted straight into the main room.

"Well, it is my fault, really. Shall I catch him?" asked Crissie.

That was all. It seemed quite uncomplicated. She too

entered Susan's flat, and as she went by, looked into Susan's face with a quiet, "May I?" They were the same height.

They walked into the main room together.

"Ah, I do like your ceiling," said Crissie, "mine's a sort of puce. I keep meaning to repaint it, but I just haven't got round to it."

The cat stood in the middle of the floor, looking at them idly. He chirped a comment and leapt on to the round table, knocking two books off to the carpet.

"They say," said Crissie, "a cat never knocks anything over unless it means to. Come here, Catty. You must return to your rightful owners."

Susan was taken with the undeniable beauty of these two creatures. It occurred to her Crissie had precisely the cat's quality, an animal quality, the good looks of an animal, which even clothing, and today's cosmetics, did not lessen.

The cat let Crissie reach him, then sprang away and trotted to the floor-length window, which he stared at meaningfully. His meow was now very loud, masculine. "Is that what he wants?"

Susan crossed over and undid the French door.

The white cat flipped himself out and down the three stairs like spilled milk, then vanished through a gap in the fir trees.

"Not even a good-bye. That's a cat for you. By the way, thanks again for bringing the parcel across the other night. It wasn't from Gerry, it was poor old Ed. I'll have to ring the agency."

Unenlightened, shopping not unpacked, Susan wondered whether she wanted the girl to go, or to stay.

By daylight she looked even younger. Her skin had no markers, not the faintest frown-line, or infinitesimal lapse.

She was moving, leisurely, back towards the corridor and the front door.

"Would you like some tea?" said Susan. "I've just made some.

"I'd love some."

"It's not normal tea – I mean, it's mint tea-bags."

"Even better."

In the kitchen, Crissie picked up a lemon, and then a lettuce, from the kitchen counter, and examined them reflectively. "The shape of fruit and vegetables is so intriguing. Everything is, really, when you look at it."

They went back to the main room and Crissie sat on the couch, kicking off her shoes so her clean, exquisite feet could burrow in the carpet. There was black nail-varnish on her toenails.

"How long have you been in this flat, Susan?"

"Not long. A month or so."

"I've only been in mine a few months too. Do you want to change a lot? Because you're an artist, aren't you? I noticed the easel and canvases in the other room."

"Sort of an artist. I do book-jackets, sometimes."

"That must be fascinating, to be able to do that."

Susan said, politely, "What kind of work do you do?" She was curious as well, she half expected Crissie to say she didn't have to work.

Crissie smiled her sweet and amiable smile. "I'm a prostitute."

The months had gone by after R.J. Foolishly, believing the propaganda, Susan anticipated constantly that the hurt and sense of desolation would ease. They did not do so.

"Susan, you seem to need a break."

"I'm sorry about not getting this done on time."

"It's okay. I understand. But well. Why not take some leave?"

Near Christmas, Susan saw his book in the display at Paragon. Then in the shops. The jacket illustration was very ordinary. She ordered a copy, but then, having got it home to Brashspeare Road, found she couldn't read it.

She put it in the bookcase with his other eleven novels, the ones he had given her, and the one with her cover. And then in the New Year, she pulled them all out and took the books to a charity shop.

But it didn't help. Of course not. Nothing could.

It was not that she thought of him, longed for him, every minute of every day and night. It was that a kind of sludgy darkness hung over her. She couldn't be happy, even in little ways. And if ever she managed to be, for a moment or so, the darkness shifted and made a strange sound in her brain, resettling itself, reminding her.

She went through stages of misery and anger, sarcasm and self-dislike. She drank too much. Stopped drinking alcohol altogether. None of this led anywhere, except back to R.J.

In February there was a party Paragon gave, and she was asked and expected to go, but he might be there, so she didn't.

However, she finished two covers on time that were all right.

Anne called and said she might come over in the summer, (alone, Wizz was always busy) but Anne had said this before at least ten times.

Anne now and then sounded old. Certainly sometimes elderly. Her voice would suddenly croak on random words. She was over sixty. Her laughter, too, was finally very American. She said, "Oh, boy, is Wizzy fat. He has to diet. What a blimp."

Susan found she was oddly shocked. Never before had Anne said anything so derogatory about Wizz.

Anne said, "So, you're still in that dump you told me about in Shakespeare Street?"

"Brashspeare. Yes."

"Look, honey, I'm going to send you some money." This too had often been said, but recently nothing much had evolved from it. "I mean, this fat guy of mine is making millions. You should see this place. Wall to wall everything. He's in Hollywood right now, would you believe it. He wouldn't take me, he says I complain. It's only for three nights, and I admit I hate L.A. I'll send you something, okay?"

This was incoherent, seemingly, but then the money came, a dollar cheque now, which Susan's bank would not baulk at, since she had for years been receiving U.S. dollars for some of her work. The bank did baulk slightly, however, because the cheque was substantial. It was for thirty thousand dollars, about eighteen thousand pounds.

What was she supposed to do with it?

Find a new flat? Eighteen thousand wouldn't be

anywhere near enough, obviously. Visit her mother and Wizz? No.

Susan had been working an extra day a week at Paragon, to make up the money for her slippage over covers. Coming back from London in March on the train, she picked up a local paper discarded on the seat beside her. She had decided to look for a new flat after all, the eighteen thousand providing some sort of down-payment. The flat in Brashspeare Road was where she had been in love with R.J.

The local paper covered an area she knew. She had lived there once, with Anne.

The carriage was fairly full. A man with a penetrating voice kept talking on a mobile phone, arch insults bounced off his (presumably) girlfriend, but it was more a display apparently intended for the uninterested and resentful other passengers.

Rain smashed into the windows, trying to get at him, but failing.

In the colour photograph, it looked a sort of salmon shade, the house, the deep green trees grouped selectively and graciously, as in a theatre set. Where the drive had been widened was an ornamental thing, perhaps a fountain.

("Yeah, Donna, I ain't saying you ain't a sharp dresser. I mean I ain't *saying* it, Donna.")

Tower Gardens. 'A fine and large house, of great character, parts of which were built prior to 1900, but all extensively modernised in its conversion to self-contained flats, with gas-fired central heating and double-glazing throughout.' Two of the sought-after flats were now on offer.

One of these was spacious, the lounge twenty-seven feet by thirty-six, and having two bathrooms and four bedrooms. The other flat was two-bedroomed, with bathroom and cloakroom, and modern fitted kitchen. Both flats had 'beautiful views of secluded communal gardens.'

She could afford neither, even with Anne's (Wizz's) money.

I'm thirty-two, she thought.

She felt old and dry. How long before her voice began to crack?

("Donna, just don't push it, girl. No," he was stern now, "just watch your mouth.")

Old enough to saddle herself with a mortgage.

Perhaps strangest of all, when told, Anne had never queried the new address, which might, surely, have rung some sort of bell with her – Tower Gardens etc: coupled with the known area. Could Anne have *forgotten*? But then, Susan had never said just which house she was thinking of living in.

Susan waited. She said, "Yes?"

I didn't mishear. I know what she said. She said she is a prostitute.

"Funny, isn't it," said Crissie, drinking her mint tea. "Actually, it's quite a good job. I mean, if you like it."

"Do you... like it? No, sorry –"

"Why? I wouldn't have told you if I was upset about it. I don't tell everyone, obviously. But we're – neighbours." Still carefree, lovely, smiling. "I'd better reassure you though, I work through an agency, and I never bring my work home."

VI

Summer came and went. Autumn arrived, turning much of the rich green of the garden to ochre and sallow red. In the autumn, they repainted Crissie's ceiling, perched up on a couple of high ladders, dust sheets everywhere, rollers, and pale peach emulsion. It was the second repainting. She had wanted to try coral before.

Crissie's flat was, Susan supposed, what might be called minimalist, but without that spindly starkness she, Susan, associated with the term.

Crissie had kept the ivory walls, hanging in the main room only two faded prints, one seeming to be Pre-Raphaelite, and one of a drawing by Mervyn Peake, representing a curious elongated child. There was also a big mirror in a black lacquer frame. The floor was the bare polished wood, which someone came in to 'do' at regular intervals, with a couple of rather tattered but glorious gold and maroon rugs with gold fringes. There were also two armchairs, narrow, old-fashioned wingbacks, in a dark coppery velvet. No couch. The French window had rough blanched muslin curtains, which at night, when the four side lamps were switched on, would hide nothing. There was also, despite the lack of noise, an involved music centre with four speakers, and a smallish TV.

This was really all.

Sometimes two tall blue willow pattern vases

manifested, holding up flaming gladioli or vermilion lilies. There were hardly any ornaments – a misted-glass apple, the slim figure of a Greek god, perhaps Apollo, nearly three and a half feet tall and done in white marble. On the polished table, of which there was only one, stood a fruit bowl that changed colour with the fruit.

It was not obviously a moneyed room. It was full of air and space and reflections, and sometimes the soft uncanny music of Debussy or Scriabin.

The bedroom, where sometimes they went to fetch something or compare some new garment, or try out new make-up, was undersea and blue, with a low single wooden bed, a Chinese chest and carved yellow wood armoire to hold clothes.

Susan admired these rooms. Their oblique colour-combinations and shapes, which worked together, and the lack of clutter. There were no awkward hung-on-to objects. No plants, even. The few books were in a case against the corner.

"I always want to change my flat after I've been in yours."

"Yes, I do sometimes after yours. But," said Crissie, "we don't, do we?"

She didn't play at assertiveness or indecision, or at anything, it seemed. Not Crissie. Even her sexual ventures with men were unfazed and unfaked. "I just *like* sex so much."

"But – even if your clients – if they're –"

"Nasty, you mean? No, I avoid nasty ones, or unhygienic ones. But anyone else is fine. I don't mind how he looks. Or if he's old. Or what he wants. Or if he's too fast. I can come –" she said, airy as her rooms, neither boasting nor apologising, "*like that.*" Her turn of phrase, still somehow old-fashioned. Charming. Unfazed

Susan also helplessly admired Crissie. For her work not the least. Though it must also be unwise and risky – and every day the media carried more horror stories of HIV and AIDS. But Crissie had even spoken about that. "The agency, G.D. – is very *good*. They try to screen everyone. We use protection. And I have a check every couple of months. Oh, it's not foolproof. I could get it, I know that."

"You're only nineteen –" That was another astonishing fact that had been established early.

"Well, I am nineteen. But even children die, Susie-Woo."

"You mean, if it happened, you would be dead-pan and philosophical about dying."

"No, not *dead*-pan. But, well, we all die sometime. I mean, you can die at seven or seventy, nine or a hundred and nine."

"You're not afraid of dying."

"Maybe. It would depend how, perhaps."

"No, I mean, you're not afraid of being *dead*."

"No such thing," said Crissie. In the lamplight, like a creature of clear glass; easy to believe she meant what she said.

"I see. You know."

"Oh, we all know."

"*I* don't, Crissie."

"You do. You've just forgotten. Look, Susie," (Susan never minded it when Crissie did things with her name) "think of it this way. You're born and you're alive. What's your earliest memory?"

"I'm not sure… "

"Well, but how old were you when you started to be aware of things that you still remember now?"

"About three, I think. I know my mother said her first memory was when she was four."

"There you are."

"Where?"

"You were alive and in the world, from nought upwards, but you don't remember it. Nothing for three or four years. So it's just possible there was something even before *nought* that you don't remember."

Later Susan had said, "Under hypnosis people can sometimes be regressed to earliest childhood. To birth even. Then they seem to remember everything."

"They sometimes remember other things, too."

Susan's first visit to Crissie's flat, soon after the New Year, had been for a meal. As in all else, Crissie was open and pulled no punches.

"I like female company, too. I don't mean I'm gay. I enjoy sex with men. But women – they're fun. And here you are. I was alone at Christmas. I don't see my parents now. And I love cooking things for people. I'm greedy and very clever. Come on, I dare you not to like my risotto with baked lamb."

Susan, drawn in during the cooking by Crissie for a glass of buttery claret, sat on a stool in the identical fitted kitchen to her own, but looking-glass effect, everything the opposite way round. She watched Crissie moving about in a huge black apron, effortlessly cutting and chopping and mixing, speaking of a hundred different things, while the wonderful scent of the food intensified.

"Taste this."

"Oh – it's –"

"You like it. Guess the vegetables? Well, guess the herbs."

"I can't – it's like everything in the world –"

"It *is* everything in the world."

They drank all the large bottle of wine with the meal, and afterwards Crissie brought brandy, and Algerian coffee in little blue cups. They had moved to the main room by then, having eaten in the kitchen at a table with an apricot cloth, with one tall church candle.

Presently Crissie put on a single short piece of music to be listened to. It was winding and serpentine. Then they talked again, then grew sleepy. It was only ten but, "Time for bed," said Crissie softly, rising without subterfuge or excuse. "See you tomorrow." They had been all evening in perfect agreement, or rather, perfect counterpoise. And it was the first time since R.J. Susan had slept really well. Afterwards, she could never remember the name of the music, or its composer, or remember to ask Crissie what they had been. Like the life before life?

They were divided by thirteen years, but like the hallway and the two front doors, this partition seemed to mean nothing. If anything, Crissie was far more mature, Susan thought, than she herself. Perhaps her extraordinary job had contributed to this, but there were other things.

Contrary to the first evening, when they had parted

after only three and three-quarter hours, there came to be nights when they sat, in one or other of the flats, talking until two or three in the morning. Or later. Once they had even both fallen asleep over a late night TV horror film, running on Susan's larger TV, and woken up at eight in the morning. Then they had breakfast, (Crissie insisting on making porridge, with oatmeal brought from 6C) like lovers.

But they were not lovers. They were – what were they? Friends? More than that.

There was a closeness, a *knowing* between them, almost from the first. No, *from* the first. Though they liked many different things, were separated by an age gap, their backgrounds, and by how they earned a living, they somehow tied up with each other, as Crissie one day, unembarrassedly said, like two gloves.

"Which is right and which is left?" Susan asked.

"Oh, I'm the sinister one."

But Crissie was not sinister. She was mild and transparent as the muslin of her sitting-room curtains, which by night showed every glowing lamp and movement in the room beyond: nothing to hide.

Susan thought, I *do* love her. And briefly felt uncomfortable, wondering if this were somehow wrong, to love a woman if one weren't gay. But why would it be? And Crissie seemed to like, to be fond of – to love Susan.

It was not that they were always exchanging touches, or hugging, though now and then, as on Crissie's birthday in November, this had spontaneously happened. They simply co-existed. Yes, that was the word. With most people you got by, you evaded or pretended, or as in the case of a man you loved, became absorbed – and the bits of you that were left outside ached in the cold. But with Crissie, with Crissie and Susan, they lived their lives together and apart, with no sense of chafing, no desire to break away or – more terribly, push closer, thrust inside.

Crissie did not even look so much the younger, nor Susan much the elder. Susan looked young for her age, and had often been taken for someone in her late twenties. Crissie of course looked older, a woman in her *early* twenties.

Though they dressed for differing tastes, they did not, as Anne might have put it, *clash* in their appearances.

Their light brown hair and pale skin were similar. And their eyes. Their height if not figure.

Nothing demanding was said by either about a filial resemblance. Sisters – no, this was not it at all. They were *not* alike in that way. Two gloves of nearly matching colours, but of uncorresponding materials, and patterned quite differently. But still, two gloves.

When they went out, usually in the middle of the week, or the odd weekend when Crissie was not working, Susan felt unavoidably proud of Crissie – "This is my friend." Sometimes men would be interested in them, and gravitate their way, sitting at the next table in the restaurant, perhaps, or picking them up in the bar or on the train after a film. They were nice to them, these men, liked their fleeting company, but never wished to develop the liaisons. Susan actively did not want another man after R.J. It had become almost cosy, this state, since Crissie.

Whereas Crissie had said privately, during one of the long night talks, those talks when the afterlife and AIDS and so on had been mooted, "It wouldn't be fair on a man. Maybe one day. I can't see it, somehow."

Crissie, (at nineteen) did not look into the future, although sometimes into the past.

"Dad was a builder. My mother – well, she was into being a Gold-Medal Mother. We were quite well-off. I went to a fee-paying school, you know the sort of thing. But – there was some trouble. I told you, I don't ever see them now. I haven't since I was fifteen."

Susan imagined Crissie meant she had discovered, under-age, the lure of sex, perhaps become pregnant, and so incurred the wrath of her parents, whose characters Crissie had not really filled in.

Crissie said, as if Susan had asked, "It was something that happened when I was a child. As Dad said, after I was nine I was fine. He said it a lot. And it rhymed, so we couldn't forget it. Mother's contribution was that bloody name she gave me." Crissie didn't sound angry, only momentarily exasperated. "Crystal. Oh what a thing to saddle a kid with. As soon as I ran off – which you won't be surprised to learn was with my boyfriend of twenty-two – I changed it to Crissie. I suppose I could have changed it totally. I think, then, I meant to keep in touch. But I had to realise in the end I never wanted to."

"Did they try to find you?"

"I expect so."

"You don't know?"

"I don't know what they did. Or do. They could even be dead. Dad worked too hard and he was a big drinker, and Mother was scared of every disease under the sun."

Susan wondered what Crissie had done that was so awful, when she was a child. She wondered if Crissie would say, but that time Crissie didn't, and soon they were speaking of something else.

One night Susan told Crissie at length about her own past. Her own mother, and Wizz, and then about R.J. Crissie sat listening, sympathetic and involved, tender, gentle and cool as rain. She let Susan recount it all, all she wanted. Sometimes Crissie said things, unjarring and so apt that afterwards Susan forgot what they were – they were the same things Susan might have said to console and reassure herself, perhaps. There was nothing judgmental or self-expanding about Crissie. She never told Susan she had been foolish, or badly-used, or that Wizz was a monster or R.J. a bastard, or what she, Crissie, would have done, or what Susan *should* have done. She seemed to have said, Susan thought afterwards, only that life could hurt you, yet here they were. But there was also the kindness of Crissie, her eyes and how they looked at Susan, and the way she brought her the glass of wine, and then touched the tip of Susan's nose for half a second with her warm, smooth finger.

Like a mother? No. Not like that. Not like any of that. Like Crissie.

There came a gloaming afternoon in late November, when Susan, walking along the Strand, saw Crissie near the Savoy with one of her clients.

Crissie, working, was not very altered from the

everyday Crissie, in appearance. Glamorously and expensively dressed, faultlessly made-up, and this time with blood-red lipstick, that on her young mouth looked only edibly correct. She was standing with an oldish, overweight man in a Savile Row suit. He was holding her hand, and she was looking into his eyes, smiling, sweet and affectionate, playful and calm. Then he said something and she laughed and he laughed.

Susan turned away and walked on. The crowd was thick and surging, it was nearly four – she had left Paragon early to pick up a book at Zwemmers.

Then Crissie was there.

"Hello, Susie. I saw you go by. That was my lovely Heinrich. We were just bidding adieu. Thanks for not saying anything. He'd be shy."

Susan knew that the deal with the clients was often to lunch or dine first, the mask of the agency being that it provided social escorts. There was one young man, Crissie said, Todd, who seldom wanted sex, only that Crissie go with him to various functions, and act "as if I can't keep my hands off him."

"Isn't that –?"

"No," cried Crissie, "it's fun, like acting in drama. I love it. He's brilliant too. We scream afterwards."

She spoke of them all undamningly. She never told Susan anything much, either, carefully not betraying them, and sometimes stressed that *this* was not the man's real name, she didn't know what that was.

"Shall we go for tea? This is a rotten time, the trains will be getting packed," said Crissie.

So they went to Zwemmers, then had tea and scones, and then Crissie got them both a black cab all the way back to Tower Gardens.

Anne rang that night, at a quarter past midnight.

"Anne...? Are you all right?"

"Sure, I'm fine. Just bored as hell. So I thought I'd call you. What time is it there? Oh. Well it's just around seven p.m. here."

Wizz was away on one of his, by now, perennial excursions. This time it was to Hawaii.

"I didn't want to go," said Anne. "I mean, take-off in winter, with ice on the wings when you land?"

They talked for a while, Susan holding the receiver away to shut off her yawns from her mother – she had been in bed, drifting, when the phone went.

Finally Anne said, "You know, I think the rat is playing around again. No, I am sure he is. He's been doing it, on and off, for years. What a skunk. Christ, I've long thought he even had the Hispanic maid that time."

"I'm sorry," said Susan.

"Not as sorry as he is when I start on about it. But God, Sue, I'm old. I'm so old. That's what it is. It never matters if you're a man. But for a woman – past fifty is shitsville."

Anne had never called her Sue. Anne perhaps, would never have said *I am old*. So who *was* this on the line?

VII

Outside the vegetable house, the vegetable trees of the maintained garden were putting on again their sticky, chestnut-red buds. A man came and gave the bench below Susan's French doors a new coat of glaucous peacock paint. Later there was a solitary blue paw mark on her steps – the autograph of one of the pet cats. Probably not the white one though. She hadn't seen it, nor had Crissie, ever again. That cold day of the bench painting, too, a letter came from Anne, the first for some time. The airmail envelope had come undone, which had happened once or twice with registered mail in the past, but the sheet of paper was not lost. Susan took it out with a definite feeling of unease.

But, to begin with, there was no fresh update on adultery or arguments.

'I'm coming over, across the Pond, to your neck of the woods, in a week, maybe two. I mean to London. It will be great to see you. This visit, let's really have a good time. Wizz says stay ten days. And cash isn't a problem. But of course I have to *earn* it. Even when he gave me those trips I took to Paris and Germany – did I ever mention those? I sent you postcards, I'm sure I did – even then I always had to go meet someone for him. Unpaid courier for the business. Although to be fair to him, I guess I do get paid, don't I. And the couple in Germany were great. Anyhow, this time is the worst. It isn't some packet to deliver this time. I have to bring this darn girl over to her father. Eve spoke to me about it, too. Eve is her aunt, or something, God knows and who cares. Obviously they don't want this brat travelling alone, so I have to be the chaperone for the trip, and I am dreading it but dreading it. Can you picture me? Stuck with a twelve-year-old for eight hours in a plane. My favorite thing. And then an hour or whatever into London. Oh well. Why don't you meet me – us – at the airport? I've enclosed details of a good cab firm Wizz knows, near London. I'll pick up the check. All you need do is call them your end. Okay? Did I ever say Eve and I had a falling out, too? The bitch took his side, I mean Wizz's side. Over this fooling around stuff. She said, men do it, I'd better put up or shut up. I'd suspect Eve of being part of the stuff *done*, only she's two years older than me, and now she looks like a crow that's been through a car-wash.'

"I'm not looking forward to seeing her. I can't help it. She says she may be here ten days. I don't know if she'll want to stay in a hotel or come out here. God – I really – I don't want to see her."

Crissie nodded. "It's difficult. Perhaps she won't stay as long as she says. Or she'll go off on her own like last time."

"I don't think she will, now. She sounded so fed up on the phone. She must be very unhappy. I feel sorry – but I still hate the idea. And I hate saying I hate it, too."

"Whyever? Why lie to yourself?"

"Don't you?"

"Not often, Susie-Woo."

"Well, who do you lie to, then?" Susan said,

unexpectedly.

She answered thoughtfully. "Men, sometimes. I have to, or they don't have the best sort of time with me. Let's see, who else? Oh, you. About your birthday present. But that's all I'm saying on that score."

Susan smiled a little. Then she said, "How is it I didn't break all contact with Anne, as you did with your parents? I mean, I only had one to get rid of, and you managed both."

"True. But then I think they really wanted the break too."

"*They* wanted it –"

"They were scared of me, Susan. I mean really scared. And even when everything was all right, and stayed all right, they kept expecting it all to happen again, despite what the psychiatrist, or whatever he was, said. Hence my dad's awful little mantra, fine after nine. It was meant to keep the devilish bane at bay. To frighten *me* into suppressing – oh anything that might bring it on."

Susan sat, watching Crissie, the twilight deepening in the unlit room.

Crissie looked down at the waxed floor, at her reflection in it. She said, "I know my mother was petrified when I began to have periods. She thought that would trigger everything again. But it didn't."

Susan undid her mouth. Then closed it.

Crissie said, "I've never told you this. It isn't that I'm afraid of myself, I'm not, although I don't understand it. Or ashamed, either, as I think I was meant to be. But not everyone wants to hear about things like this."

A swift nausea wriggled through Susan's stomach and mind.

What had Crissie *done*?

"This was the thing you said happened when you were small."

"Yes. The daft thing is, I don't remember any of it. Well, not much. Do you remember when I asked you what your earliest memory was, and you said around three, or four."

"Yes."

"Well I don't have – how shall I say – *proper* memories, not until I was nine."

There was silence.

Susan held the coffee cup, which had ceased to mean anything, though half-full. Crissie sat quietly, looking down into the lake of her waxed floor. She seemed as ever serene, perhaps just a little melancholy. And all around the grey-blue shadow bloomed like fog.

"Had there been an accident?" said Susan at last.

"Amnesia? No, it wasn't that. Nothing happened. My mother had a perfectly ordinary pregnancy, gave birth, according to Dad at least, without much bother. It was a quick birth, he said, only a couple of hours from start to finish, they barely got to the hospital in time. And I was a healthy six pound baby, just a week early."

The silence began again. It was like a noise, a recollected noise, but of what?

Beyond the arched French door, so reminiscent of Susan's, the blue-grey garden sank into the space and oblivion of night.

"You see, I say I don't have real memories, but I do have a type of memory. From the beginning, I think. I'm not sure, I never have been."

And silence again.

This time it went on and on.

"Crissie, if you don't want to talk about this, please don't."

Crissie looked up. Across the silent blurring of all things, her eyes shone, clear and feral as a cat's, but colourless as a cat's never were.

"I'm concerned that you might rather not hear."

It was true. The hair moved slightly on Susan's scalp. Suddenly, though she had never thought of it, or no more than once, before this hour, she recalled that they sat in what remained of the sunken rooms of the insane metamorphic house of her grandmother.

"Maybe you're right, I don't want to – but – look, can I put a light on?"

"You know you can."

Susan got up. As she crossed the room she blundered against the table with the fruit bowl. The tangerines leapt and rolled away. "Sorry." Then the light came on to her touch. The room moved from nothingness to a golden magical normalcy. Even Crissie's books gleamed in the bookcase, the beautifully illustrated fairytales, and books of photographs of India and Egypt, the Shakespeare in red and the Chaucer in black.

Crissie had also got up. She switched on the three other lights.

She turned back in her dancing, dancer's way. "It's still me, Susie." It was not a plea, not a challenge. Only an absolute.

"Yes, sorry. That was just sitting here in the 'tween-light, greeking of auld ghoosties, or whatever."

"It wasn't a ghost," said Crissie. "It was a poltergeist." She stood on the floor, on her reflection. "Look, here it is. No sooner did they get the baby – me – home to their posho house in Kent, than things started to happen. At first not every day. But then, every day. The things that happen with poltergeists. Psychokinetic activity. Lights blew out, furniture moved dramatically, pictures flew off the walls, even some of the windows broke, apparently. My parents would hear banging noises, knocks and thumps. My mother said on one occasion something had mowed through the dining-room carpet – as if a lawnmower had gone over it, she said. My mother was the one, you'll gather, who made sure I had all the details as soon as I was 'old enough'. At first, when it started, they tried to *ignore* it. They got panicky. They attempted one or two solutions, which achieved nothing. Then they found this man near Harley Street. He explained about the phenomena. He said this happened sometimes round young children, even adolescents. He said it would stop. But they still had six and a half more years of it. And then – then it did stop. By then they'd got well used to it. Which meant Dad drank and went out a lot, and my mother was on tranks. The au pairs regularly left, too. Well, they would, wouldn't they?"

"Yes," said Susan woodenly. She said, "This was in Kent?"

"Marion Hill, Kent. Yes."

"And you don't remember –"

"What I remember is this. A kind of blaze without colour or light. Being furious and frustrated. I remember walking and walking through a sort of – well, I thought, when I was older, it was a kind of train tunnel. The light there was very faint, but I could see, and I wanted to get somewhere. Only I didn't get there. And of course, how could I be walking in a tunnel like that, it must have been a recurring dream. I remember striking at things too – what things? I don't know – but it made them shake, only I don't think I did it with my hands. I remember being lonely in a way I never have since. I remember being in the dark."

Again silence. The light flickered in the lamps, but sometimes that happened here and elsewhere. The lamps might flicker as the electric grid was overloaded, or the power source changed over.

"My first distinct, logical memory," said Crissie, "is of my father saying to me, You've been a good girl. And I didn't know what he meant, but my mother nodded, I can see her now, nodding. And I felt pleased with myself for being this Good Girl. The poltergeist activity hadn't happened, apparently, for a month, which till then was unheard of. My father said, Now you can have that bike I promised. And I didn't know what he was talking about. But you see, I understood language. I'd learnt how to talk and walk. I could even read and write, rather well actually. I just couldn't recall how I'd learnt any of it. Like I didn't recall the paranormal stuff that seemingly I'd caused until it stopped and I was a Good Girl, and earned the bike."

Susan said, "There was a poltergeist here, in this

building, before it was converted into flats. So I've heard."

Crissie glanced at her. She looked intrigued not dismayed. "Really? I know they crop up here and there. Mine wasn't the only case."

"Why did you take the flat here, Crissie?"

Susan heard the churlish, Inquisitional note in her voice. Perhaps Crissie didn't.

"The agency found it for me. They're really helpful that way. I was living in Highgate but I wanted a bigger place. They sorted it all out. I just moved in. That was the first time I saw the flat."

What is it?

Look at her. She's twenty years old now. She looks it tonight. No make-up, her old sweater that cost perhaps only a hundred pounds. Barefoot.

No it isn't anything.

A coincidence.

It could all be rubbish, lies, anyway. She could be a total fucking romancer. Even all this about her job – whore – how do I know? All I know is what she's told me. And that one man I saw her with – some rich old sugar-daddy – even, for God's sake, *her* daddy, the builder. Her money comes from somewhere, but why from working at anything? She's out a lot, so she goes out a lot.

I don't know a thing about her. Have taken her on trust, like I take everyone. Ghastly useless selfish Patrick and conniving oh-so-genuine R.J., and my bloody slapper of a mother, who is the real hooker, if anyone is, lapping up Wizz's dollars, first in exchange for sex, then in exchange for keeping quiet about his sex with all the little Madisons.

Christ, this *sounds* like my mother, like Anne, as she is now.

I feel like her.

I am not Anne.

I am me.

And Crissie?

I don't know what the fuck Crissie is.

"Crissie, look, I'd better go. Thanks for telling me. But I shouldn't have stayed so long – I've got to organise a few things, if Anne's coming."

Crissie smiled. Nothing to it. Unfazed. Knowing.

"Yes, Crissie, it did sound a bit weird. Sorry. But."

"It's okay, Susan. I've got some washing to do anyhow. I'll see you tomorrow."

She has conned me.

She is the con artist.

Lulled me and listened, and been lovely, and then told me her ghost story and made my skin crawl –

In her own flat, Susan switched on all the lights. Then she pulled the wire out at the telephone point, afraid the phone would start to ring and ring.

The driver wanted to chat all the way to Heathrow. He began by asking Susan where she was flying to, though she had no luggage. Then, when she said she wasn't going anywhere, he commenced asking in-depth questions about who she was going to meet, where they had come from, why they were here – it was, Susan thought (inaccurately) like an interrogation.

She had felt already tired and depressed when she got into the cab. Walking into the terminal, where the crowds swirled over endless floors, she felt drained – by the crowd, the space and its synthetic smell, the dull morning light, the cabdriver, her mother, everything.

Is she going to recognise me? Perhaps I should hold up a card printed with my name or hers.

Then another thought, worse. Will I recognise *her*?

It was a long wait.

Sourly, the thoughts pressed home. What are we going to say to each other? *Do* together? (I could have introduced her to Crissie – the gush of pride – "This is Crissie, my friend –" But that was out of the question, now. Susan had been avoiding Crissie, and Crissie made no overtures. Susan... didn't know about Crissie.)

(Or anything.)

When Anne finally came through, Susan started almost in alarm. For Anne looked just as she had always done. She wore a well-cut navy suit, not even seeming at all crumpled. She was tanned, eyes and lips painted, her shortish hair a sheer bold white. Her nails were pale gold and on her hand flared the emerald. She carried one small suitcase, a piece of hand luggage and her American purse.

"Anne – you look wonderful!" Susan cried in a shambles of shame. And even as she said it, having now come near enough, she saw that the suit *was* crumpled, a very little, that the white hair was too dry, the brown skin creased, the mouth too bright. And with this too-bright mouth Anne leaned forward and kissed her, hugging her in the bony embrace, leaving a lipstick mark Susan could feel on her cheek, and had to wipe away surreptitiously. Anne would never have done that, not even last time – but ten, twelve years had passed. Had it really been so long?

"God, I am exhausted," said Anne. Her eyes were not very clear, she looked half-cornered with irritation. "What a goddam bloody flight. Turbulence – delays – how late am I?"

"About two hours."

"Christ. That was the other thing. My watch stopped. Wouldn't you know it? One year old from Tiffany's, and it stops. This is Delores."

Susan looked where her mother off-handedly indicated. Susan had forgotten the annoyingly foisted twelve-year-old child who had had to fly in with Anne.

Delores had a honey skin with large black eyes. Her soft dark springing hair was tied in two long plaits. She wore a jumper, ski-jacket and jeans. She did not, Susan thought, look like a child, at least not really like an English child – or not like any child from Susan's childhood. Not like Susan, of course, not at all. Susan, at twelve, would have envied Delores her spotless complexion and slight figure, possibly her pierced ears and the little gold studs.

Delores did not smile. She seemed bored and evasive, her eyes shifting off from Susan. She didn't bother to return Susan's greeting.

"Is the cab waiting?" said Anne. "Good. Let's get the bathroom, then I need a drink."

Anne had been drinking already. She smelled of alcohol, again something Susan didn't remember from before. Even after her nights out, Anne had never smelled of anything other than cleanness and scent, or perhaps a partner's cigarettes.

In the bar, Anne had a double vodka tonic. Susan had a white wine spritzer. The child, when asked what she wanted, said, "Coke," untainted either by please or thank you.

"Is she all right?" Susan said to her mother, when Delores suddenly got up and walked away. She didn't go far, only to a fruit machine, at which she stared.

"Depends on how you class all right," said Anne. The drink had freshened her. She sounded less husky. Face to face her U.S. accent was hardly noticeable, except on certain words – class, God, and so on.

Delores meandered back. She looked at Anne, looked away. "I wanna dollar change."

"Dollars don't work over here, Delores," said Anne, briskly. "Eve gave you some English money at Kennedy, didn't she?"

Delores blinked. She didn't open her own small purse, a buckled denim creation.

Anne said, "She forgot then. What is it you want?"

"I wanna play that."

Susan said, "Here, have this."

When Delores had gone back to the machine, Susan said, "She seems a bit –"

"She *is* a bit. Oh boy, is she. A brat, I said."

It was a relief to be able to have the child to talk about.

"Maybe she's just nervous. She's Eve Frenowsky's niece?"

"Something like that. Look, she's got the darn thing working. But it won't cough up, so she's hitting it –" Anne called across the bar, nearly stridently, "Delores, lay off!"

To Susan's surprise, Delores turned a fixed, somehow bleached face to Anne. She nodded swiftly. She looked terrified.

"Funny kid," said Anne. "I can't make her out. I tried to talk to her, asked her if she was excited, coming to see her father. She shook her little head. Well, I guess she's been over before. Eve says they're separated, the parents. Rich as hell." Anne shrugged. "But she is a bloody graceless child. But then kids are."

"Are they?"

"Wait till you have one."

Susan said, "I have waited. I don't want children."

Anne said, "Sensible."

Susan thought, Is she going to say, *I wish I never had*?

But Anne only said, "I asked him to come, you know."

"Wizz."

"Yep. I knew he'd say no, and he said no. I have a feeling he is all set for a mad fling while I am over here. Some nubile eighteen-year-old. Or why stop at only one?"

"Do you think we ought to go and find the cab – he's been waiting so long."

"Yeah, I guess. This vodka is crap. That is one of the many benefits of the U.S., decent food, decent booze. And the vitamins, what you can get there. And the treatments."

Susan went over to fetch Delores from the fruit machine. She hadn't won anything. She was the sort of demanding ungiving child you expected to win.

"We're going out to the car now, Delores."

Delores glanced at her, away. Any fright at a raised

voice was gone. But she left the machine without demur.

The driver didn't chat now; he seemed to expect them to converse with each other, and so perhaps entertain him and feed him information.

They all squashed in the back, the child wedged uncomfortably in the middle like a thin bolster.

"Eve said she has to sit there, and the window seat on the plane. She doesn't like other seats."

This seemed strange, for if Delores wanted to be by the window in the plane, why not the window in the car?

Susan felt uneasy, as they breathed wine and vodka over her, talking across her inert dark head. But then, Anne had already baptised her in this, no doubt, during the flight.

"I can't wait to see London," said Anne. "It looks so small and old."

Then she leaned back. She shut her eyes which were overlaid by shadow and a mascara too black for the aging tan and the white hair. The knuckles of her hands had enlarged. Probably now she could never take off Wizz's emerald ring, even if she wanted to.

Susan gazed from the cab window, watched miles of concrete streaming past, houses and trees and a succession of disturbingly big, low planes.

When she turned to her mother again, she saw Anne had fallen asleep, her mouth slightly open.

Susan's heart sank lower. She felt wounded, *defiled*, by Anne's decay. She felt – embarrassed by her.

Then she remembered her childhood – Anne, in the bath, or varnishing her toenails. Susan wanted to cry.

But she was too old herself for that.

And then Susan thought of pouring all this out to Crissie, and how Crissie would be, kind and tender, encouraging and interested, philosophical, never saying the wrong thing. Helping, wonderful Crissie.

But there could be no more indulgence in Crissie, who might after all be a dangerously crazy liar-lunatic.

I never told Crissie about Catherine, Susan thought. Everyone else, but not my grandmother. I nearly did, when she was going on about her poltergeist nonsense. Nearly then. But I didn't.

The suburbs trailed by. Susan thought of being hurried, always late, to the house on Sundays. She thought of Catherine standing there, that last time, straight and hard and ruined.

She could see Catherine now again, in the face of Anne.

The journey didn't seem to take long. There was a lot of traffic rumbling the same way, to London, but no significant hold-ups.

"Look, there's Big Ben," said Susan, stupidly, to Delores. Who took no notice.

But Anne gave a little snort and woke up.

"God. Was I asleep?"

"I think so," said Susan. "You must be tired."

"I don't get that jet-lag stuff," said Anne stubbornly. "But I guess I'm tired." Then she seemed to shake herself together, sitting up, moving her hand over her hair, redoing her lipstick in a car-jolted compact mirror.

"Okay, Delores, we'll be there in a minute."

Delores moved vaguely on the seat. Her mouth

looked sulky, her eyes almost moronic.

"Where does Delores have to go – I mean where is her father meeting her?"

"It's an address I have here, off Whitehall. I told the taxi."

A few minutes later, they turned into a street of large, flat-faced terraced buildings. Broad stone steps, guarded by stone lions with heraldic shields, led to glass doors whose handles glinted cold gold in the muddy sun.

"Impressive, your daddy's office," said Anne.

"What number was it, madam?"

The taxi crawled to a halt.

At that instant the child glanced again at Susan. Delores' face was a total blank. Perhaps there really was something wrong with her mentally. The great black eyes seemed to have no one in behind them, not a child, not a person, no one at all.

Unnervingly, before Susan could get out of the cab to give her access, Delores scrambled unheedingly over her. Anne was already on the pavement, and took the child's hand firmly. Susan could picture Eve saying, "You have to hold her hand on the street."

"It's okay, Sue. I'll see to this. There's the doorman."

A porter had appeared. Anne conducted the child up the stone steps, and spoke to him. A snatch of Anne's voice, over the traffic noise, said a foreign name, (not Frenowsky, Susan thought) something she didn't quite catch, or afterwards recall.

Anne and the child went through into a plush, black-carpeted lacuna beyond the glass doors.

Unexpectedly, the driver didn't start to chat now,

either. Susan had assumed he would break loose again, if he and she were alone. Instead they both sat there, dumbly waiting, he with his back to her. Minutes went by.

Susan said, "Perhaps I ought to –" But exactly then Anne came out of the swing doors alone.

"Thank Christ that's seen to. Someone came down in the elevator. *Not* the father, mind you. A big guy in a suit. Well, he looked like a bouncer to me. But he knew about Delores. He was very pleasant to me. She just took his hand like a lamb. You know, little bitch, she was all goofy smiles for *him*, flirting away."

"Where to, madam?" said the driver.

"Oh, take me to a decent pub," sighed Anne.

Susan was unsure, but the driver said, "What about the Royal Lion, just around the corner there. Nice enough place, and quiet."

So they drove round to the Royal Lion.

Anne paid the driver in cash, (he did not offer to assist with Anne's luggage) and the cab moved slowly off, ahead of two big cars that had also pulled into the street.

The pub looked shabby to Susan. It was not very clean, but there was picturesque sawdust on the floor and old, dark green pots with deadish plants in them – perhaps things the driver thought an American might find quaint. A few people drank at tottery tables. Through a doorway there came a rap of balls in a pool game.

"Shall I get some sandwiches?" Susan asked. "If they do them."

"If you like," said Anne. "I'm not hungry."

But the Royal Lion did not do sandwiches, only bags of crisps and peanuts. Susan thought Anne would be able to get something to eat when they reached her hotel, something to soak up some of the alcohol.

As Susan brought the drinks back to their own rickety table, a tall man in a leather jacket came in from the street. She noticed him for a second because, though younger, he reminded her faintly of R.J.

"Cheers," said Anne. "That's English enough, isn't it?"

Susan laughed falsely. "Oh, yes."

Anne swallowed some of her drink. "I've had enough," she said.

"Well maybe if we eat soon –"

"No, Susan, I don't mean the booze. I mean I have had it with him. I have had it."

Susan cleared her throat. She wished she were not so conscious of the man like R.J., somewhere behind her. R.J. was not what she needed to be reminded of. And not now.

"You mean Wizz."

"Yes. Who else. I am going to leave Wizz. Oh, I haven't told him yet. He thinks I'm all set to go on clinging tooth and claw to our non-existent relationship. But I am not. No way."

"What will you do?"

Don't, please *don't* say you will move back to England and live with me.

Anne parted her enamelled lips to tell Susan what she would do, and instead of elaborating, looked up in surprise. The shadow lay over their table. It was the man like R.J. He wasn't like R.J. There were three other men, casually dressed, well-built, and a woman in fawn slacks and a cashmere sweater.

The man who was not R.J. had something which he was showing them, some sort of I.D., like a plain-clothes policeman.

"Get up, madam."

Anne's face was furious. "What the hell is this? What the fuck do you want?"

The man leaned over and pulled her to her feet, and Susan found she too stood up at the same time, as if some cord connected them. And Anne seemed to struggle, and the woman in the sweater was there. She spoke softly. "You and the young woman come with us now, and quietly. Or we can cuff you and drag you out. Which?"

Outside the sun had gone in. The two large dark cars waited with open doors. This was a dream.

As Anne was 'helped' into one car, and Susan into the one behind, Susan tried to speak. "Save it," said the man who wasn't like R.J. Then she was sitting crushed between two of the other men, just as Delores had had to sit between herself and Anne.

During the hours when she stayed in the steel-white room, she thought it through, and saw the shape of it. *Having* seen, Susan saw that it was obvious. She should have known. Anne should have known. Or had Anne known? *They* thought so. Or – did they?

A uniformed woman sat at a small table in the corner. First she ate a bar of chocolate. Then she took another one out of a drawer in the table, and ate that. Later, much later, she took out another, and ate that too. Each bar was of a different make.

The light was too bright. There were no windows, and they probably locked the door, although Susan wasn't sure; she never attempted to open it. Once she asked for the lavatory. They made her wait nearly half an hour, then another woman came and took her to a toilet of three cubicles just along the passage. "Leave the door open." So Susan left the cubicle door open, and sitting pissing in front of this other woman, who did, actually, turn her head slightly away, Susan remembered the awful bathroom in Wizz's loft, with its two pally lavatories done in matching black and gold.

At other times, a man and a woman questioned her. She supposed that was what they were doing. They were not any of the men, or the one woman, who had taken Anne and Susan into custody at the pub. The man had gingery hair and a freckled scowl. The woman looked French, a delicate and sharply-made brunette. But she spoke with a slight trace of a Scottish accent.

"Where's my mother?"

"Don't worry about your mother."

"Of course I am. What have you done with her?"

"The same as we're doing with you, Miss Wilde."

"Why am I – why are we here?"

It turned out they were there because of Delores, that brain-dead, rude and graceless child, who, with the man from her father's office, had become melting and friendly.

It turned out too that Delores' attitude and manner were undoubtedly the product of her intense conditioning, over a period of time, to know who must be made up to, and who must not. Also, of course, to a fear and horror and misery beyond anything such a child should ever know.

As it came clear to Susan, she was racked not only by her own leaden fear and panic, and her appalled concerns about Anne, but by remorse. The very young girl Anne had brought from JFK to London was no relative of Eve's, no daughter of a rich friend of Wizz's. She was one of those lost children, there to be taken by stealth or connivance from the sinks of most cities, warped and worked into the appropriate consistency, then flown out like refrigerated flowers to any destination that could pay.

She wasn't the first *commodity* that Anne had 'delivered' for Wizz, and therefore for the firm. Anne, the paid or unpaid courier. What had those things been in the past, the thing she had had to take to the Georgian manor house near Brighton, the *packets* for Paris, and Germany. Illegal smuggled jewels or art treasures? Hard drugs?

They imported everything, the firm. Anne had said that once. A joke? Imported and exported.

Susan, as she put the pieces together, began trying to explain them to the people who talked to her on and on in the steel-white room. They were already aware of them, naturally.

"My mother didn't know – she's been duped. He's used her."

Basic psychology. Wizz wanted to get rid of Anne. He hadn't known she'd planned to leave him. So if she were caught – too bad?

Susan grasped *he* would be safe away. Already she could tell this operation would have been far reaching. There would be others working on the other side of the Atlantic, to trap Wizz's firm. But most would escape. Wizz always would.

He's a gangster.

She had sensed it at sixteen, and Anne had not. But then, Anne was in love with him. What could Susan say she had known about R.J., really known? Love was blind, or blinded itself.

Had Anne, *had* she known? No. Anne, for all her crash into age and unbeauty and vodka, was not that kind of woman who could consentingly bring a kid of twelve to England to become the sexual toy of some wealthy group or outfit of paedophiles. Was she. Was she?

"Do you think *I* was in on this?"

"Well, Miss Wilde, were you?"

They must have tapped Anne and Wizz's phones. They would have heard conversations between Anne and Susan. Did these people suppose it was all done in code, in case?

After they had photographed Susan, searched her – so shocked by then, numbed, she barely noticed this search, carried out by an expressionless woman, but wondering if there would be an internal search – there was not – then later wondering if Anne, the courier, had been – a woman of almost sixty-two – subjected to one – after they had done these, and other matter-of-fact, intrusive things, some of which Susan only recollected hours later, Susan thought, They do think I'm guilty of this. And Anne is guilty.

But she kept trying to persuade the gingery man and the svelte Scottish woman that neither she nor Anne was guilty at all.

Susan told them about Wizz, and what she knew about Eve. It was so little.

She supposed they would not catch Eve, either. Perhaps not anyone from the firm.

And so Anne and she might have to do.

"What time is it?"

She thought the chocolate woman might not answer, but she glanced at her watch and said, "Nine thirty-five." They had taken Susan's watch away, along with some of the things in her bag. If this was expediency, or another form of coercion, she did not know.

Some unmoist cheese sandwiches had been brought, and some tea. They had let her have a glass of water, too.

"I don't know what I can ask you," said Susan, "what am I allowed to ask?"

The chocolate woman looked at her.

"When can I see my mother?"

The chocolate woman said," I wouldn't hold your breath."

"She isn't young," said Susan. Even in this extremity, saying that, she felt disloyal. "I don't think she's very well."

The woman nodded. The nod meant nothing.

At one a.m. Susan asked the time again. And at seventeen minutes past one, when she asked again, the ginger man, the Scottish woman, and another man –

fat, with glasses – came in.

Susan got up.

"Let me see my mother, please."

"I'm sorry," said the fat man. He sounded sorry, apologetic, not unkind, which seemed unbearably threatening now, or had Susan only watched too many shows on TV?

"At least tell me if she's all right."

"Quite all right. Rather distressed, of course."

Susan suddenly found she was crying. She sat down. The tears ran across her face and stopped. She wondered, removed and bleak, were tears a show of innocence to these people or only of culpable fear?

The fat man came over and pulled out a chair and sat sidelong to her. The ginger man stood. The woman perched on the larger table, across which all dialogue had previously been lobbed.

"This hasn't been pleasant for you, Miss Wilde. I know that. And I'm sorry to tell you there will be charges brought against Anne Wilde, your mother. Personally, I'm of the opinion she's merely been incredibly naïve, but at the moment not everyone is happy with that. I suppose rank stupidity could be counted as an offence in a case like this."

Susan felt void. It was like the last stages of a virus. She didn't care anymore. She said, mechanically, "Will the child be all right?" Because in the distant future she might sometime want to know.

"Perhaps."

"I thought –"

"Oh, we've got the child away from them. There won't be any more of that for her. But I'm sure you're aware, in these situations, certain things will already have happened. She'll be damaged. They always are. But, she's young. As you are, Miss Wilde. We heal better when we're young."

Beyond the room, a bell rang, once, twice. It sounded almost like a fire drill, but no one took any notice.

"There's just one other matter I need to mention, Miss Wilde." He waited, as if for her to say brightly, *Oh, what*? Then he said, "Your friend at the flats, Crissie Fielding –"

Susan thought, Who is Crissie Fielding? She thought, But they will have watched me, too, they know everything. They probably know what I have for breakfast. They probably know my whole life story. They know I have a neighbour who is unhinged, and called Crissie.

"What about her?"

"It seems she has some influential admirers, Miss Wilde. We wondered a little, you see. But she isn't someone who would need to be involved in this sort of dirty little game."

"You thought Crissie –"

"No, we didn't think anything, Miss Wilde. Nor do we think it about you, you'll be relieved to learn. And now that's sorted out," (what had been?) "maybe we should get you home."

Susan started to say, in her viral voice of halting cotton wool, "You must let me see Anne first –"

But nobody took any notice.

The fat man went out, smiling and affable, his work, whatever it was, well done. Susan had to sign a couple of papers. They took her down to another room and gave her back her watch and the things from her handbag.

Then she had to sit and wait, and now she didn't know why. Unless it was all a ruse, and they weren't going to let her go.

In this room, which was bigger, with pale, grey-washed walls and more-padded chairs, and an unoccupied desk, there was also a clock.

The clock and Susan's watch showed almost an hour's difference. Obviously it would be her watch which had gone wrong, slowing down in captivity as she had.

And she thought of Anne somewhere in the building, (as if she had only just realised this) her own watch useless, and should Susan have made more fuss? But no, it would accomplish nothing.

She thought, What do I have to do? Do I have to get her a lawyer? Maybe Mike Hammond, or Laurel, could advise her. She would have to talk to someone. It was all such a business. She remembered Anne saying, soft and sombre, "Oh, God, now we've got all this death business, forms, mess, and the bloody funeral." After the police found Catherine sitting dead on a park bench, twenty years ago.

It was five a.m., or four-ten. Someone came in, a man. "Come along, Miss Wilde."

She followed him, and they went through a lot of fiercely lit corridors, and at the windows, which any new room they passed had, the black sky seemed never likely to give way.

She fell asleep in the car, as Anne had, during the drive back into London. The driver woke her in a side street. Here she had to leave the big car and get into a cab. She was cold. She thought confusedly the cab driver would start to talk: Where have you been? Where are you going this time of the morning? He never spoke.

She wondered if she had enough money on her to pay him. This grew frighteningly important. She started to elaborate mental plans of how she must explain, leave him what cash she had, rush into her flat and bring the rest out. In the end, he pulled up in Dunkirk Street, where now the trees were large and fine and covered with the spearheads of buds. It was so cold. Something like white sugar coated the gutters, the roofs, the limbs of boughs. She got out, but the cab drove off before she could begin the rigmarole about money.

In the early morning, with the milk-floats going by, under the thinning sky, where light had broken through the blackness after all, in the smell of the cold. Walking.

Why hadn't the cab brought her to Tower Road? They would have had to come by another route. Was this to cause more disorientation? Or a mix up?

Over fences, creepers had shawls of ice. Would the park gates be closed? No, they were open. Someone was collecting litter. A bird sang shrilly from the direction of the public toilets.

But the grass was all slathered in brittle white. It crunched under her shoes. And then people hurried past her, off to catch the early trains, and she thought of Anne, left behind. And she thought of Anne.

As she let herself into her flat (6E) Susan recalled she had gone by Crissie's flat across the hall, (6C) and hadn't seen it, as if it were not there.

Had she gone by the statement about Crissie like this, too?

What had the fat man said? What had he implied? Crissie had influential admirers. Presumably men she had slept with, in her trade as a prostitute. So, what she had told Susan about that was a fact after all, not a fabrication.

But also – also had the fat man been saying that they had investigated Crissie, and to protect Crissie, or her 'admirers' – they had left Susan herself ultimately alone? Or did he mean that Crissie had somehow learned what had happened, and asked someone, some admirer, (Heinrich maybe, Ed, or Todd) to intervene at a high level and save Susan's skin?

Why? Why would Crissie – why would she care so much?

The curtains stood open at the arched windows, undrawn last night.

Beyond the French doors of the main room, as on the drive leading to the house, lawn and trees were frosted white.

Susan found she had switched on the central heating. It made a knocking, tapping sound. She walked up and down across the room, trying to be warm again. Should she make tea? Pour a measure of brandy? The decision was beyond her. It was like the time after R.J.

In the end, she went to the French door, unlocked it, let the icy air come slicing in. She didn't know why she did. She didn't understand at all. None of it.

On the recently painted bench to the left of the steps something was.

Susan turned to see.

Someone was sitting on the bench.

Susan looked.

It was the figure of a woman. Slender and straight, with loose fair hair – or hair that had been loose and fair.

"Crissie...?" said Susan.

The woman sat there, on the bench. Her skin appeared monochrome, nearly colourless. Nearly sepia... her clothes, her hair, these were covered with the white lace of the frost, which at the edges of her garments, hair, had turned to a crochet of white. In profile, one eye of dark grey crystal – that seemed daintily fractured as if by a flung stone.

But it was Susan's eyes that had fragmented, one pane sliding across another.

She was back in the past of this living, metamorphosing house. The face she saw was not dead, but only mummified with its bitterness.

"What is the point," said the old woman in the pumpkin house of Susan's memory, "of my being alive? There you are, the two of you," (She means me, and Anne, my mother) "flesh of my flesh, the children of my body, there you are, and I am alone. This is what I have come to." It had been her fault, and perhaps she had realised that. Was it tears in her eyes? All that poison and tactless cruelty – made of regret and tears. We hated her, were allergic to her, Susan thought. As now I dislike and dread my mother.

Catherine. She had died. There in that cold park. And after that she had haunted this house. Not as a ghost, but as a poltergeist expressed from the body of a baby that became a child, miles off. In Kent. (I knew in her flat that evening, in the twilight when we put the lights on – and that's why I've avoided her. Not because I thought she was insane. Because I saw what she'd told me – was true.)

As someone had said, Catherine hadn't known she must go away. Rather, she had thought she must return to her house. And return she did in the only way she then could. Years of fascinating the cats in Jackie's rescue centre, terrorising grumpy Mildred with knockings, opened windows, hidden things, distressing Olivia and Jeremy's trendy existence. Only finally settling into her reborn physical self at the age of nine: Crystal, the daughter of a wealthy builder and his gold-medal wife. And Crystal's life was to be as different from the life of Catherine as Crystal could make it. Until fate, or her burning inner will, manipulated the world, and brought her again to the vegetable house. After which, Susan knocked on the door of her flat.

Catherine had wanted love from those two who never loved her. Only this second time, one of them had.

Catherine sat on the blue bench, covered in the frost of her previous death, living now, but demonstrating how it had been.

Catherine. Who had become Crissie.

Crissie turned. She turned her head. The frost came with her lightly, like a veil. It was in her fringe, on her eyebrows, lashes. It was over every inch of her. But the grey crystal eyes were not fractured, only webbed, and they saw. She looked at Susan and smiled her ice-rimed, frozen, triumphant smile of grey glass.

About the Author

Tanith Lee was born in North London (UK) in 1947. Because her parents were professional dancers (ballroom, Latin American) and had to live where the work was, she attended a number of truly terrible schools, and didn't learn to read – she is also dyslectic – until almost age 8. And then only because her father taught her. This opened the world of books to Lee, and by 9 she was writing. After much better education at a grammar school, Lee went on to work in a library. This was followed by various other jobs – shop assistant, waitress, clerk – plus a year at art college when she was 25-26. In 1974 this mosaic ended when DAW Books of America, under the leadership of Donald A Wollheim, bought and published Lee's *The Birthgrave*, and thereafter 26 of her novels and collections.

Since then Lee has written around 90 books, and approaching 300 short stories. 4 of her radio plays have been broadcast by the BBC; she also wrote 2 episodes (*Sarcophagus* and *Sand*) for the TV series *Blake's 7*. Some of her stories regularly get read on Radio 7.

Lee writes in many styles in and across many genres, including Horror, SF and Fantasy, Historical, Detective, Contemporary-Psychological, Children and Young Adult. Her preoccupation, though, is always people.

In 1992 she married the writer-artist-photographer John Kaiine, her companion since 1987. They live on the Sussex Weald, near the sea, in a house full of books and plants, with two black and white overlords called cats.

Lightning Source UK Ltd.
Milton Keynes UK
08 April 2011

170588UK00001B/44/P